MAHALAS LANE

a novel

MARIANNE CUSHING

Cover design by Paul Rodino
Cover photo by Doug Landreth
Spine photo by R. Scott Schmid

ISBN-13: 978-1493791316
ISBN-10: 1493791311

PRINTED IN THE UNITED STATES OF AMERICA

For Gene and Taryn,
who are my heart and soul.
Thank you for unselfishly sharing me
with Mahalas Lane.

Acknowledgments

This novel has been a five-year journey and without the following people, *Mahalas Lane* would still be collecting dust in my laptop. First and foremost, the brilliant and generous Gwen Moran, whose tireless advice and unconditional friendship are priceless. Michelle Priestley Lunt of Islandport Press, who gave me hope and introduced me to my amazing editor, Melissa Hayes, who made a real author out of me!

I am forever grateful to each of you.

PART ONE

CHAPTER ONE

The sun certainly rises early on Owls Head, Kay thought as she awoke to its stabbing rays. It was one of countless reasons she loved living on the coast of Maine.

This was the ideal place for her to call home, especially here on quiet, pebble-lined Mahalas Lane. A scattering of houses surrounded hers on this scarcely populated corner of the peninsula, and Kay Andrews reveled in the solitude. When she relocated from down coast three years ago, her ultimate objective had been to escape her ex-husband, Bill, a man who'd sadly taken far more interest in the bottle than he had ever taken in her.

The 1970s A-frame house was an incredible deal. A former vacation rental, it had been on the auction block for substantially less than it was once worth. While its misfit architecture and massive state of disarray stood out like a sore thumb among the charming shingled cottages of her neighbors, it was financially attainable, and had ocean access. After all the combative years she had spent living with Bill,

Kay viewed the battered structure as a reflection of her own state of mind, and was determined to return both to their original glory.

Mornings here were her favorite. It was the quietest part of the day, when even the rowdy vacationers next door were undetectable. When she had first bought her home, the old Walker cottage to her left, with its unusual boat shaped facade, was just another dilapidated structure she'd passed on her way down the sloping lane. Like much of the Northeast, Owls Head had taken its fair share of hits in the recession. The fact that the cottage next door was abandoned had suited her just fine, for it guaranteed her privacy. Kay's failed marriage had thoroughly exhausted her, and she was anxious for a little seclusion. Since moving in, however, the Walker place had been renovated and become a summer vacation rental.

The streaming sunlight served as Kay's daily alarm clock, beckoning her to set out on her morning walk. Looking back, she's certain she would've paid double for the house just to ensure that she'd own the narrow track of land across the lane that came with the property. It was a mere five feet wide but offered up a direct path through the wildflowers and over a wall of rocks toward the lane's private beach. The narrow parcel was sandwiched between the beautiful gray waterfront cottage across from her and the larger chunk of beachfront land belonging to the Walker cottage next door.

The neighbor's chunk of waterfront access was much wider than hers, large enough for a boathouse, a small lawn, and some flowering landscape. It wasn't uncommon to see such unusual property lines on Owls Head, particularly on roads leading to the water. In many cases, homes could be built directly on the coastal side of the street; however, topography sometimes dictated that houses be erected farther from the rocky shore. For these homeowners, their properties continued across the road, giving them access to the beach.

Kay would walk the beach during the early hours of the morning while the tide was at its lowest, when the water kindly shifted far enough out to expose a wide, sandy shoreline. As the day progressed, the punishing waves would begin to swallow the sand until they worked their way up to the shelf of slippery, seaweed-covered rocks. Upon her return she would stop to admire the flower garden she'd planted next to her mailbox before going inside to brew her morning coffee, pausing to speak lovingly to the perennials, urging them to open their petals to the sun. When the sun set each day, her flowers would clam up into a protective huddle, the irony of which was not lost on Kay. She was quite aware that she had shut herself off from almost all human interaction these past few years, except for the hours she worked as a waitress at the Black Bull Tavern. In fact, she'd been downright unapproachable lately, particularly to the stream of curious vacationers who constantly interrupted her gardening.

She dreaded their endless questions about the area, the lighthouse, and where they should eat. *Good Lord, people—get a travel agent!* she would scream inside her head. Eventually, Kay learned to avoid eye contact with them, even if it meant she would later overhear them complaining about her unfriendly demeanor while they sat on the pebbled front patio of the cottage.

As she walked the beach this morning, she enjoyed the sunlight sparkling on the small ripples of Penobscot Bay. The water was mostly calm, although not quite the smooth, glass-like shelf it would become later, in the evening.

According to her routine, she reached the sand where her rocky ledge turned into beach, made a sharp left, and walked to the end of the curving C-shaped peninsula as far as the smooth sand would take her. She strolled past the only three waterfront homes at the end of her lane and came to a pile of huge rocks where the last house stood. Situated at the end of another winding lane, these rocks anchored their small beach.

She turned back around and faced the boathouse of the Walker cottage and the few large homes to the south of her path. Those houses were built far up and out on their properties, appearing almost suspended in the air to take full advantage of the water views. Stunning views aside, she had always wondered why those owners would build their homes on a parcel that never had a low-enough tide to create a sandy beach. The only way to the water for them was down a long, treacherous pile of rocks.

To her left offshore was a large, uninhabited island that loomed like a shadow in the dark. Like many of the thousands of islands off Maine's coast, this one was only accessible by boat. She had kayaked there once when she had first moved in, but the wind and current had made it a daunting task, one she had yet to repeat. In truth, the island looked a lot closer than it actually was. As her gaze returned to the rocky coast, she spotted a pair of beady eyes staring at her.

Great, she thought. *That pesky dog again.* Sure enough, bounding straight for her was the same golden retriever she had seen the past couple of weeks. She was surprised to see him today because she was certain he belonged to the rabble-rousers next door. She had even called last week to complain about the dog's barking to the rental agent. Yet she had seen them pack up and leave the day before.

She quickly turned toward home to avoid having to pet the overly friendly ball of caramel fur. As she did, she gasped and stopped short, almost crashing into a tall, silver-haired man who stood before her.

"Mornin'," the man said.

She grumbled a reply, irritated at the interruption in her morning walk.

"It's mine," he stated.

Thinking the stranger was referring to his dog, Kay was just about to inform him that there was a leash law in Owls Head when he lifted his arm, and the shiny silver cleat he was holding came crashing down on her skull.

CHAPTER TWO

"Excuse me . . . pardon me," Madi Lyons repeated as she wormed her way through the crowd of students. *Don't the teachers see me trying to get through this crowd of oblivious, giggling girls?* She'd been passing by this all-girls Catholic school for more than half a dozen years, and the navy plaid skirts and white button-down tops with round collars always reminded her of the traditional uniform she'd worn as a child.

This was the first parish to be named St. Patrick's in the city, predating the renowned Fifth Avenue church. This neighborhood in Chinatown used to be largely Italian, and after living in Manhattan a while, she had learned from locals that Martin Scorsese had once attended this school. Madi loved living in the city for various reasons, including its diverse history and its infinite opportunities.

She flew down the twelve dirty, familiar steps and into the tiny dining room of her favorite lunch spot, Wo Hop. She knew Kristen would be furious, having been kept waiting for nearly thirty minutes. Madi had told her best friend that it wasn't a good time to do lunch since she was leaving tomorrow for vacation, yet Kristen had insisted on meeting, saying it was important, and that Madi's deadlines could wait.

Kris doesn't know what it's like to have eight different creative teams vying for the same account, Madi thought, *or how easy it is to be knocked down a rung or two if the client doesn't choose your campaign.* The advertising business was cutthroat in New York, and she had to be at the top of her game. After all, she was thirty-two already, and time was ticking. She had to work hard if she wanted to make her mark. She believed that if she didn't make it to creative director by forty, she would be washed up.

Madi tried to erase the look of disappointment on Kristen's face with a big smile and a quick smooch on her friend's cheek. She plopped into her seat, shoving her coat behind her on the wooden bench. Peering at her from either side of Kristen's pouting face were her favorite autographed photos of Derek Jeter and Barbra Streisand, hanging on the star-studded wall.

In an instant, the ever-dependable Chai was standing beside her with her tea, nodding and saying hello. "The usual, Miss Madi?" he asked.

"Yes, thank you, Chai," she replied.

"What's so important you couldn't tell me on the phone?" Madi asked, "or by text or e-mail?"

"You know, Madi, not everything in life should be shared via electronic device," Kristen replied disapprovingly.

"Are you sick?" Madi asked, concerned.

"No, I'm not sick. I simply have some very important news, and I wanted to see your face when I told you," Kristen announced with a smile.

Chai had appeared and silently set a bowl of soup in front of her.

"Did you get a promotion?" Madi asked, slurping up her first taste of egg-drop wonton soup. She was certain there was nowhere else in Chinatown (or the world, for that matter) that made it so well. This basement dive was a local treasure, as evidenced by the number of patrons in suits and uniforms at every table.

"I'm getting married!" Kristen exclaimed, proudly holding up her left hand.

Madi dropped her spoon and it clinked twice across the shiny red Formica table before falling to the floor. Her mouth agape, she mustered an enthusiastic if a bit disingenuous "Oh my God, Kris, that's awesome!"

* * *

Thank heavens she had more than seven hours in the car until she arrived in Midcoast Maine; she would need that much time to get over Kristen's news. She also wanted to have the full experience of driving up the coast so that she could feel a million miles away from Manhattan.

Madi knew it was selfish to feel the way she did about Kristen, her best friend since third grade. She should be happy for her; actually, she should be ecstatic. Yet what she really felt about it was a sense of loss, the same feeling she'd had after her father died. Less than a year after her father's death, her mother had remarried and moved south with her new husband, also a widower. While she was happy for them, she was an only child and missed having her family nearby. Kristen was the sister Madi never had. They had been together through thick and thin—boyfriends and broken hearts, college days, moving to the city, starting their careers. It was all part of their big plan to be successful together, the two of them conquering the world.

Kristen would now be half of a married couple, making polite excuses as to why she couldn't go to a show or get a drink after work, or even share their regular trips to the gym. Madi had been through it with other friends who'd fallen in love and gotten married, their single lives gone forever. Madi knew that with married life came married friends. With one quick sip of soup, she had gone from partner-in-crime to third wheel.

When she was a kid in Westchester, in one of his rare sentimental moments, Madi's father had told her that she could do anything she wanted in life. He'd told her that she was smart enough to pursue any dream. Undeniably old-fashioned, her Catholic Italian father believed a woman's place was in the home, caring for her family. But to his daughter, he said, "You're different, Madi. You're not cut out to be a housewife."

In her head, she knew he'd meant it as a compliment. It was his way of encouraging her to go to college rather than rush to find a husband and settle down. Yet, there was something about it that had made Madi feel she wasn't marriage material. She and her father had often butted heads, and she felt he was being facetious. When he said she should have a career, she thought her dad was really saying she was too independent to land a man. Her insecurities became a source of low self-esteem with men, which she masked well with her unwavering determination to succeed in her career.

As the landscape changed from honking cars and highways to rolling fields and oak trees, her stress level diminished. By the time she hit I-95 at the northern coast of Massachusetts, the smell of salt water coming in through the slightly open window brought with it a wave of relief. Kristen, the agency, and the pressures of the concrete jungle would have to wait a week, because she was less than two hours away from a much-needed escape. Rolling down all four windows, she blasted the car stereo and inhaled the fresh sea air.

CHAPTER THREE

This was the third call the sheriff had received in the past two months about a disturbance on Mahalas Lane. It seemed the boathouse at the old Walker cottage was turning into a local teenage hangout. The property had been renovated last year, and now the small outbuilding near the water had a new wooden porch on the east side, beyond the view of the main cottage. He assumed that some kids were hanging out on the beach again, and a couple of lovebirds must have snuck into the single-room boathouse.

It was the first time a call had come in to the ten-person department during the morning; the others had been at night. The caller, a resident from the next lane over, had said he'd heard a dog barking incessantly; he thought he might have even heard a scream.

When the sheriff pulled his patrol car to a slow stop in front of the cottage, he saw a rental car in the driveway to his left. He kept the car running but turned off the flashing lights, so as not to disturb the guests. He headed away from the main house down to the boathouse. Since it was only seven a.m., he assumed the renters would still be sleeping. Perhaps he could scare off the trespassers in time to depart before anyone noticed his presence. He unlatched the green wooden gate and walked across the small lawn toward the steps of the boathouse porch.

Owls Head was by no means a vacation mecca, but there had been a noticeable change in recent years. Once, this small town had rarely welcomed visitors, other than the occasional lighthouse fanatic who had done enough research to know there was one on the peninsula. It was the expansion of the Knox County Regional Airport—specifically, commercial aircraft flying in from Boston and New York City twice daily—that had put this unknown town on the tourism radar. City people had historically summered in other, "more desirable" areas of the northeastern and New England coast. However, these days Long Island was dirty, Cape Cod was packed, and Nantucket was overpriced, opening the door for tourists to take another look at the coast of Maine.

Sheriff Joshua Daniels of Owls Head had lived in Maine his whole life. Having come from a long line of shipbuilders and seamen, his father was more than a bit disappointed at his decision to go into law enforcement rather than engineering at the Maine Maritime Academy. While he had grown up in the neighboring town of Rockland, his great-great-grandfather had once built ships at the long since defunct Adams/Brown shipyard near Owls Head Harbor.

On the other hand, his mother, curator at the Wyeth Center in Rockland, was proud of her son's election, and bragged daily to museumgoers that her son was the youngest sheriff ever elected in Knox County. It was typically anything but a dangerous position, since this community had one of the lowest crime rates in the country. Other than occasional code violations, like bonfires on the beach or noise coming from rental properties, it was mainly a figurehead position. His attendance at town meetings and community events was the backbone of his job. Lately, assuring residents that the influx of tourists could only benefit the small town and its economy was his top priority. He had a natural-born gift for making people feel reassured. In fact, his high school nickname was "The Mayor," thanks to his people skills and ability to diffuse tense situations.

The sheriff didn't see anything amiss at the boathouse, nor did he see any trespassers, so he walked to the crest of the path. It took just seconds to notice the prone figure of a woman down on the beach, just to the right of where he was standing. As he approached, the black color of the sand near the female victim's head indicated that she'd lost a great deal of blood. He knew immediately that she was probably dead. He checked for vitals, and finding none, lifted the victim's arm to check for stiffness.

Still warm and limp, he recognized Kay Andrews, resident of Mahalas Lane.

* * *

1942

"Oh my goodness, Tom! It's so beautiful!"

"Do you really like it?" Tom asked proudly.

"It's perfect," Margaret whispered. "Just like you."

"You're the one who's perfect," Tom insisted as he took his new bride

in his arms.

Tomorrow, he would go back out to sea for months. He was relieved to have finished the cottage in time. With such a rough winter this past season, and the record-breaking snowfall, he hadn't been sure he could pull it off. He'd been determined, however, because his wife was expecting their first child. The house was his gift to her. He had built their new home in the shape of a boat, to remind her of him during the long periods of time they would be apart.

* * *

Madi was standing at the shoreline, picking up flat stones and trying to skip them. Every rock hit the water with a *plunk,* only to disappear beneath the sleek surface.

"Ugh!" she groaned in frustration. She heard him chuckle behind her.

"Like this," he said, tossing a stone with ease. One, two, three, four, five, six times across the water before disappearing.

How did he do that? She marveled at his rock-skipping talents. "You make it look so easy," she flirted.

She subconsciously became aware that she was dreaming, and fought her body's attempt to wake up. She shut her eyes tighter, forcing herself to remain asleep. She was standing close enough to feel his breath as he wrapped himself around her, demonstrating how to hold her arm properly. The sun was now shining so brightly, she had to shield her eyes. She held her arm up to cover her face, and the sensation of waking came over her again. She fought to prolong her delightful dream with this handsome stranger. She didn't want it to end.

"Hello . . . hello . . ." her dream man said over and over.

Was she not paying attention to him? What was happening—and what was that infernal knocking?

As her eyes slowly opened, she saw what was blinding her. The morning sun was coming in through the porthole that served as her bedroom window. *So bright,* she thought as she unwillingly emerged from slumber.

"Hello! Is anyone home?" a man's voice called.

Madi sat straight up as she realized the voice was coming from outside the cottage. Apparently, the man was also knocking on her door.

"I'm coming!" she yelled, propelling her petite body off the antique platform bed and onto the cool hardwood floor. "Be right there!" she added, quickly glancing in the oval mirror above the white tallboy. Running her fingers through her hair and tugging on a T-shirt, she scurried through the living room to the door.

The main door was actually on the side of the cottage. This was because the front of the house had an unusual rounded shape, like the front of a boat, covered across the bow with windows that lifted upward and attached to large brass hooks. As she reached the door, Madi could see a police car parked on the narrow lane through the front windows.

What the hell . . . the police?

She opened the door to an officer standing on the front step, beyond the cottage's outer, screened door. The secondary door had a carved sailboat in the middle of a wooden frame, with screening above and below it. Through the center of the sail, she could see his hand resting on his belt, atop his gun. Feeling uncomfortable in her pajamas, she greeted him through the screen.

"Yes, Officer—is there a problem?"

Really, Madi, she chided herself, *of course there's a problem. He's standing here at this ungodly hour holding his weapon. It's certainly not the welcome wagon.*

"I'm Sheriff Joshua Daniels. May I come in, miss?" the officer inquired, flashing his badge.

"May I ask why?"

"There's been a disturbance on the beach, and I need to ask you a few questions."

Her New York wariness now at full pitch, she reluctantly opened the door and took a step back to allow him entry, jumping as the screen door slammed shut behind him. Madi watched as he scanned the kitchen to the right, the living room to the left, and then the small hallway.

"May I have your name, please?" he asked.

"Madi Lyons."

"Are there any other guests?"

Hesitantly she replied, "Just me."

She felt completely undressed as she stood there in just her pajamas while he looked her up and down. She couldn't see his eyes through his mirrored sunglasses, but she was certain his glances weren't standard police procedure, and she tensed. He caught her eye as she glared at him and he quickly averted his gaze.

"What's going on, Officer?" She was getting irritated, wishing she were still in bed, dreaming.

"We received a call early this morning about some noise on the beach. Did you hear anything?"

She shook her head and replied with skilled sarcasm, "Nothing—other than you banging on my door."

He ignored the comment and proceeded with his questioning. "When did you arrive in Owls Head?"

"Yesterday afternoon. Why?"

He returned her question with another. "Can you tell me what you did last night?"

"I drove to the general store for a few things, brought back a pizza, and then went for a walk on the beach," she said, hands folded across her chest. She was growing impatient, and tremendously uncomfortable standing in front of him braless.

"And what time was that?"

Feeling increasingly defensive, Madi said, "Officer, umm, Daniels, can you please tell me what this is all about?"

The sheriff came clean with the startling news. "A woman's body was found on the beach this morning."

A body—as in, dead? "Oh my God!" she gasped, covering her mouth.

"So I'm asking you again: What time were you on the beach last night?" It was his turn to be impatient.

"About nine-thirty," she replied, her tone much more cooperative this time.

"And this morning?" he continued.

"I was sleeping until you knocked."

"And you didn't hear any noises at all?"

"No, sir—nothing," Madi said, in disbelief.

"Okay, miss. If you remember anything, or notice something unusual, please give me a call." He handed her his card, saying, "Sorry to wake you. And please keep your doors locked."

As suddenly as he had arrived, he was gone. The slam of the screen door shook her nerves.

She wondered if the woman had drowned, or if a murder had been committed . . . *on her beach.*

CHAPTER FOUR

By the time Madi had emerged from the tiny first-floor bathroom, she could see out the front windows that a crowd had gathered, including an ambulance, the medical examiner, and a small group of looky-loos. She exited the house out of the rear laundry-room door and went to grab a bike from the clapboard barn in the backyard. Maybe a good long ride would take her mind off the commotion.

At the foot of the drive she turned right, avoiding the people on the side of the road. She followed another curve to the right and began to ascend the sloping lane. She passed the only three houses on the left and the two on the right, and thought again how small the people-per-square-inch ratio was here compared to Manhattan. On this tiny street alone they could fit thousands of people with a few new high-rises.

At the top of the road, she again made a right and began to accelerate her pace. Overhead a plane was making its descent into the regional airfield. *Oddly close,* she thought as she instinctively ducked her head. When she reached the main road in Owls Head, she went left toward Rockland instead of taking the right that would have looped her around the peninsula, passing the general store she had visited the night before.

It took her until late morning to begin to unwind. A cup of strong espresso and a scone at the combination bookstore and coffee shop, followed by an hour in an overstocked antiques shop on Main Street, was a great start. After going to an early matinee of the original *West Side Story* at the village cinema, she was feeling much better.

As much as she loved the movie, Madi had preferred the stage play ever since Kristen had starred as Maria in their high school rendition. She hadn't been expecting her friend to audition, since Kristen was completely oblivious to both her stunning good looks and her sweet singing voice. It was her first audition, and she'd nailed it. Madi laughed at the memory of the confident competitor's face when Kris's name was announced for the lead role. It was obvious that out of the two vying for the role, Kristen was made to play Maria, with similar olive skin and even darker brown hair than Madi's. Megan, on the other hand, was redheaded and freckle-faced— not exactly ideal characteristics for the Puerto Rican sister of the leader of the Sharks.

She hummed the tune of "Tonight" as she grabbed a lobster roll at the outdoor café stand and strolled down to the harbor, just steps from the village center. She'd have to come back with her good camera, she decided as she leaned on the rail and gazed at the dozens of lingering boats. She snapped a few shots with her cell phone. *They're like lost souls out there drifting in the water.* It was a serene and beautiful sight.

She remembered the carved sailboat in her screen door and reflected on the symbols of Maine life all over the cottage.

The blue throw pillows on the sofa embroidered with shells, the set of white butter dishes with the red lobster motif, the watercolor paintings of rocky beaches and lighthouses, and the lantern-style light fixtures in the kitchen, to name a few. Charming, and so far removed from the modern style of her beloved Manhattan.

* * *

1962

Tom tried his hardest to comfort his wife as she sobbed in his arms.

"Sweetheart, it's the best thing for him," Tom said in a soothing voice.

"He's our son, and I'm sending him away," she cried. "What kind of mother does that make me?"

He nodded. "I know it feels that way, Margaret, but he's more than we can manage, especially when I'm away. He needs professional help."

Margaret already knew all of this. The doctors and psychiatrists had explained it time and again. The local school system was fed up, and could no longer handle his unpredictable behavior. The neighbors were afraid to let their children be around him, and he had "accidentally" killed more than a couple family pets.

Yet even the thought of putting fifteen-year-old Thomas Jr. away in a "special school" was cruel, Margaret thought. Certainly the nurses and attendants wouldn't care for him and love him like his family did. And what would being sent away do to his already fragile mental condition?

She knew she had no choice. Their older daughter Sarah was nineteen, and was frightened of her brother. There had been times years ago when Thomas would gather rocks and hurl them straight at his sister as she ran down the beach. Lately, her son had taken to sleeping in the boathouse, which Margaret didn't object to because, admittedly, it made her feel more at ease at night.

When she and her husband had first told their son about the school, he was furious. First, he'd simply hidden in the boathouse, barely coming out for days. Then he'd begun to beg them, telling them he would be better if he could just stay at home. That morning, the day he was meant to leave, he'd just sat at the picnic table out front and stared down toward the ocean, his gaze as distant as the sea itself.

Margaret was heartbroken. Tom would be leaving again soon, and it would be just her and Sarah alone in the house for another long winter. With visitation to the school limited to once a month, she was afraid of what might become of her tormented child. She had no idea how she would ever forgive herself for agreeing to this.

She wiped her tearstained face and walked out to the patio to try to explain things once again to her only son.

* * *

A murder on Owls Head? Josh couldn't believe this was happening. If it were true, it would be awful for the town. The residents would be shaken up about this for a long time to come. And who, on his safe little peninsula, would murder this woman?

What he knew about the victim was that she was in her late forties and divorced from her ex-husband, a lobsterman from Boothbay Harbor. Kay Andrews had moved here to start fresh and get out from under his constant begging to take him back. What Josh hadn't known was that Bill Andrews was a drinker, and could get a little heavy-handed with his wife when he was intoxicated. After questioning some of the onlookers, Josh had learned that Bill had been to Owls Head recently, trying once again to win back Kay's affection.

Josh would head over to Boothbay Harbor later that afternoon. About an hour south of Owls Head, the harbor was known for having the largest fleet of excursion boats on the coast for viewing lighthouses, seals, islands, puffins, and fall foliage. Originally a fishing camp, deep-sea fishing cruises for cod, mackerel, tuna, haddock, and striped bass were now wildly popular. The harbor's capacity to hold hundreds of vessels made it a profitable location for lobster and seafood companies. Being the summer season, Josh knew he'd be battling crowds of tourists.

He put out an all-points bulletin on Bill Andrews in the surrounding towns of Rockland, Rockport, Thomaston, and south, along the coast to Boothbay. He was Josh's prime—and only—suspect at this point.

Since there were seldom cases like this in Midcoast Maine, the medical examiner set aside her scheduled work and started her postmortem on Kay Andrews right away, as soon as the forensics team had finished their investigation on the beach. Josh stayed in the cold examination room as long as he could stand to watch. According to her findings, the cause of death was blunt force trauma to the skull using excessive force. *Proof that it was indeed murder.* Due to the shape of the wound, the weapon clearly wasn't a rock, as Josh had originally assumed. The autopsy revealed traces of metal, so it had to be something else, like a hammer.

Before he headed down coast, he decided to see how the investigation at the victim's house was going, and to inspect the perimeter of the area once more. While there, he would also check on the renter next door. She certainly had to be shaken up by this morning's disturbance. He thought it might comfort her to know that this was most likely an isolated domestic violence incident, and that she needn't be worried—especially since she was alone.

* * *

It was after three p.m. by the time Josh got back to Mahalas Lane. He checked in with his detectives, and they reported that nothing had been disturbed in Kay's house. *Not a surprise,* he thought. He figured that Bill had come to the house first, and when he found she wasn't home, he'd walked down to the beach to look for her. They must have started arguing, and then he'd hit her. Hit her hard. He must have already been angry with her when he'd headed to the beach, because he had brought something with him—something hard and heavy enough to kill her.

There was no answer at the rental cottage next door, so Josh followed the path down to the beach. He took one large step up onto the boathouse porch, skipping the middle step, and saw her sitting in one of two blue Adirondack chairs. Her feet were up on the porch's railing, crossed at the ankles. When she didn't move, he noticed that the book was open on her chest, and her eyes were shut.

He hesitated while deciding whether he should retreat before she awoke. This would be the second time in one day that he'd woken her up. *Not a good first impression—or second,* he thought to himself. Then: *Why are you worried about making a good impression?*

He had to admit she was extremely attractive. He was afraid she'd caught him staring at her when he had entered the cottage that morning. He had tried to play it off by glancing around the room like he was doing a room check. He wasn't sure if he'd covered it well enough. He couldn't help it; she'd looked kind of sexy standing there in her Yankees T-shirt, men's boxer shorts, and long, tousled hair. In fact, the boxers were what had made him think there was a man in the house. He also thought it was pretty amusing to see a Yanks shirt here in Red Sox country.

"What the . . . ?" she gasped as she awoke to find someone standing over her. She grabbed the book as it slipped from her lap and struggled to lean forward in the reclining wooden chair. Josh also reached out to catch the book, and as he bent down to help her, their heads collided.

"I'm so sorry, Miss Lyons," he exclaimed.

She grabbed the book and stood up in front of him. "What were you doing standing there?" she demanded.

He stumbled, "I was, umm, just stopping by to, uhh . . ." He pulled himself together and finished. "I came to inform you that we believe the incident on the beach was a domestic violence situation, and not to worry because we are almost certain that the suspect has left the area."

Madi furrowed her brow and thanked him for letting her know, adding, "You know, you have quite a way of making an entrance." Her tone was less than warm, and he noticed it immediately.

"I apologize for waking you again," he said sincerely. "Let me officially welcome you to Owls Head. I hope the rest of your time here is most enjoyable."

He held out his hand, and out of obligation she took it. As they shook hands, she looked up and noticed his eyes for the first time. This morning, they'd been hidden behind his sunglasses, but now he was facing the lane and the afternoon sun was illuminating his eyes. They were shockingly blue, and the bright blue sky only added to their intensity. His eyes, along with his firm handshake, caught Madi off guard as she held onto his hand a little longer than customary. After a few more seconds, he released his grip and took a step back to leave. Once again, he was gone before she'd had a chance to reply.

What is it with this guy? she thought.

CHAPTER FIVE

1963

Augusta Mental Health Institute,
formerly Maine Insane Hospital

"We have a new patient arriving today—Thomas Walker Jr. He has just turned sixteen and comes to us from Maine State Prison. He has antisocial personality disorder. He was convicted of the first-degree murder of both of his parents, and is taking lithium and undergoing shock treatment therapy. Here is his chart and treatment schedule. Nurse Colley will be assigned to his case.

"That's all for today."

* * *

That bitch thinks she can do better than me, Bill thought. *I'll show her. When she sees how much money I'm making, she'll regret ever leaving me.*

"Eddie—another," he commanded, holding up his glass. The cash from his last lobster haul was neatly organized into piles of bills on the bar.

"Here you go, buddy," said Bill's favorite bartender, placing the new drink away from the money to avoid getting condensation on it. "Looks like things are going better, huh, Bill?"

"Yup, my man, this is my year. Things are lookin' up."

Bill carefully placed a rock on each pile of cash as the breeze picked up in the harbor. The outdoor bar of the Lobster Dock had long been a regular hangout of Bill's. No one bothered him here. No greedy lobster bosses, no nagging women, and no kids. Kay had always wanted kids, but he'd told her straight up that he was not the kid type. She had opened her smart mouth one too many times and told him he couldn't father a child if he tried. Boy, did that piss him off. That was the last time he had laid one across her big fat mouth. The next day she was gone.

As much as he hated to admit it, he missed the woman. He had even gone up there to Owls Head to tell her. But she was a stubborn one, and he knew it would take more than some half-wilted roadside flowers to get her back. This money would do the trick; he was sure of it.

"How's it going, fellas?"

Bill hated when tourists tried to talk to him at the bar. If he wanted company, he would've brought his own. He turned his back to the man and sipped his drink.

"That's a lot of Ben Franklins you've got there."

Bill responded without looking up. "Fuck off."

"I just want to ask you a few questions, Mr. Andrews," said the persistent stranger behind him.

Bill lifted his head to see a uniform standing over his left shoulder. *What now?* Couldn't be his lobster license; he finally had that squared away. And last week he'd paid the car registration, so his driver's license suspension had been lifted.

"I'm Sheriff Joshua Daniels from Owls Head," said Josh. "I'd like to ask you some questions about your wife."

"What's she sayin' now? I haven't touched her."

"Now what would make me think that you've touched her?"

"I'm tellin' ya, she's fulla shit. Must be that piece of garbage she's been fuckin' around with from the restaurant where she works." Bill was sounding a little agitated, but kept his back to the sheriff and his head in his drink.

"Sir, when was the last time you saw your wife?"

"Ex," Bill retorted.

"When was the last time you saw your *ex*-wife, Mr. Andrews?"

"What's it to you?"

"Where were you early this morning?" Josh continued.

"On my boat," Bill answered. "What lies is that bitch tellin' you now?"

"Can anyone verify your whereabouts this morning?"

Bill's waning patience could be heard in his voice. "Only the fuckin' lobsters, Officer. Now, do me a favor and go back to fuckin' Owls Head. You're talkin' to the wrong guy."

"The wrong guy for what, Andrews?" Josh persisted, although he knew from experience not to piss off a drinking man. He only had a matter of time before this got ugly, so he had to act fast. He had already called in the local sheriff's department for backup before he'd arrived in Boothbay Harbor, but he wasn't sure how quickly they would get here.

"If someone pushed her around, she prob'ly deserved it. She don't know when to shut her trap. But hey, it wasn't me."

This guy is a real piece of work.

"Sir, what exactly could your wife say to you that would merit having her skull bashed in?"

Josh was surprised at the look of horror in the man's eyes. When Bill started to push back his stool, Josh immediately went into action. He reached out for Bill's left arm and ordered, "Don't move, Mr. Andrews."

Before Bill knew it, he was pressed against the bar with his left arm behind his back, feeling the cold hard familiarity of a handcuff.

"What the fuck!" Bill shouted.

Josh heard the siren behind him. Backup had arrived—a relief, since Bill was not a small man. He was certainly strong enough to kill his wife with a single blow.

On the drive back to Owls Head, Josh kept replaying Bill's reaction in his mind. Usually he could read people, especially when they were lying. The man's expression was undoubtedly one of surprise, which didn't add up. He had to be a great actor to pull that off. *Or one sick bastard.*

* * *

This was the most excitement Josh had seen around here in years. He was spent.

He headed home, knowing that the department's crime scene investigator would be done at Kay's house and the beach by now. The tide would have washed away any remaining evidence where the body had been discovered.

He called Town Hall on his way into Owl's Head to see if anything more had been discovered. His dispatcher informed him that no murder weapon had been found. Three area residents had been questioned, and all of them had heard a dog barking, but only the caller had reported hearing a scream. No one had actually seen anything, nor did anyone know whose dog it was.

While normally Josh would take 73 all the way to North Shore Drive, this time he turned right on Dublin Road just after crossing the waterway and took the long way home, so he could canvas the crime scene area one more time. When he reached the corner of Dublin and Ash Point, he turned right instead of left, then left onto Mahalas Lane.

Madi Lyons was sitting at the wrought-iron table in front of the cottage. In her right hand she held a glass of white wine. Josh could see that the bottle was almost full, indicating she had just opened it. The sun had long since set, leaving the sky a deep twilight blue, the color it became just before it turned jet black. The candle burning on the table was a citronella, a sign that perhaps the renter had discovered the mammoth-sized mosquitoes that made their home in Maine. Next to lobsters and puffins, the third most popular tourist T-shirt sold in town featured a giant mosquito with the words STATE BIRD emblazoned on it.

He pulled to a stop in front of the cottage and rolled down his window. "Good evening, Miss Lyons."

"Good evening, Sheriff," she replied.

"Everything okay here?"

"Just fine," she said with a nod.

"I just wanted to let you know that we've got the suspect in custody, so you shouldn't have any more disturbances."

"That's great. Thank you," she said, lifting her glass in relief and gratitude for the good news.

"Okay, well . . . have a nice night."

Even in the darkness, Madi could see his blue eyes, and without thinking heard herself say, "Would you care to join me for a glass of wine, Sheriff? I'm sure you could use one."

As he exited his squad car, Josh removed his belt and placed it on the front seat before shutting the door. Naturally, the revolver, nightstick, and Taser hanging from his waist made people uncomfortable. After Madi showed him to the bathroom so he could change out of his uniform, they sat back outside at the table.

"I can't drink alcoholic beverages while in uniform," he had explained. He always carried a set of street clothes in his vehicle in case he wanted to go shopping or visit a friend after work. Accepting her offer was completely out of character for Josh, who kept his job very separate from his personal life. He rarely drank anything but green tea or water in public. At home with family and friends, he would occasionally have a beer or glass of wine. However, after the day's events, he knew he could use a drink. Plus, he couldn't deny his attraction to Madi.

By the end of their first glass, the stars had begun to pierce their way through the darkness. Madi had learned that Josh (as he'd insisted she call him) was also the current resident of the cottage at the base of the Owls Head Lighthouse. The lighthouse, built in 1825, had been converted to an automated "keeper"—a VM-100 fog detector—in 1989. While the light station itself belongs to the United States Coast Guard and abuts a state park, the original light keeper's house is a historic landmark owned by the city of Owls Head. When the light became automated, the city decided the only keeper's house of its kind in North America would be better protected and preserved if it was occupied by the reigning sheriff instead of the Coast Guard. It was Owls Head's own supreme residence.

Josh told Madi it was not as glamorous as it sounded, as the lighthouse now had more than ten thousand visitors annually, and was anything but private. The upside was that his police car parked outside did help to prevent vandalism, and kept visitors pretty well behaved. His favorite part of living there, he told her, was getting to do his stair routine to the top of the light every morning and late at night, when the park was closed.

"When there's no fog, the stars from the top are so close you can almost touch them," Josh explained.

"That sounds amazing," Madi marveled. "I'd love to see it."

"You'll have to come by one night and I'll take you up." She smiled in response.

Josh coaxed her into taking a stroll down to the beach to stargaze. "I haven't walked down this beach since I was a kid," he told her.

"Except this morning, right?"

"Oh yeah, that's right." At that moment, the morning's events seemed forever ago.

The only thing he'd focused on since they'd begun talking was Madi. She'd poured a second glass of wine for each of them, and their conversation turned to her fast-paced life in Manhattan. Her job at one of the largest advertising agencies in the world sounded fascinating, and much more exciting than his life here in Maine—even though Josh was perfectly content living in his small town. There was something genuine and pure about Madi, even though her fiery spark convinced him she could take very good care of herself in New York City.

"You can't see stars like this from my place," Madi said.

"Do you live in an apartment in the city?" he asked.

"Yes, I live on the Upper East Side—in the eighties," she said.

Josh had never been to New York City, and didn't know the eighties from the twenties. When he looked confused, she added, "I was lucky enough to find an affordable apartment in a nice, quiet neighborhood in Manhattan, if you can call any neighborhood in New York quiet." They both chuckled. "It's not fancy—it doesn't even have an elevator—but it is rent-controlled, so I'm not moving anytime soon."

"What floor?" Josh asked.

"The fourth," she answered, "so I have my own version of a stair routine."

They stood in silence as they both thought of how differently they lived, only a few hundred miles apart. It was only when Madi let out a muffled yawn that Josh looked down at his watch. They had been talking for more than two hours. The time had flown by.

"I should go," Josh said. "I have to be on duty at six tomorrow morning."

"What time is it?"

"Ten."

"Already?"

He nodded in reply and she apologized. "I'm so sorry; I didn't mean to ramble on when you have to get up so early."

"No, really, I enjoyed it," he assured her. "It was exactly what I needed." *Oh God*, he thought. *That was a little over the top.*

They walked back up the path, and when Josh got into his car, an awkward silence fell upon them both. Josh was the first to speak.

"Thanks for the wine, Madi—and the company."

"Anytime, Sheriff." She smiled.

Josh gave one last wave as he drove up the lane.

He's cute, Madi thought as she watched his car disappear beyond the neighbor's bushes.

She was reminded of her early post-college days with Kristen. New to the city, they had both been anxious to start their careers. They had a motto when it came to dating: "Catch and release." It was their way of reminding each other to remain focused on their goals while still having a little fun. Although Kristen had long since abandoned the philosophy, Madi was still not convinced she was ready for a relationship. *Would she ever be?* she wondered as the screen door slammed behind her.

CHAPTER SIX

2003

It was the first time Tom Jr. had seen the world outside the hospital courtyard in more than forty years. He still couldn't believe he was free. A casualty of chronic state budget cuts and changing philosophies about the care of the mentally ill, they had simply closed the hospital and released the two hundred remaining residents. Since hospital staff had long since lost track of his sister, his only relative, they had simply handed him his clothes, his meds, and a hundred dollars, and wished him luck.

"Please stay on your medicine, Thomas," his nurse had said. "You will be much happier." He actually thought he saw a tear in her eye.

Many years before, the shock therapy had ceased when it was determined to be cruel and torturous. He actually missed it sometimes, for between treatments he had experienced lucid moments as he had in his childhood, when he'd been himself and could see the truth. In later years, they had numbed him with so much medication that he'd felt lost inside himself.

Shortly after killing his parents, his sister Sarah had come to see him.

She was crying like a baby and asked him why he had done it. He told her to shut up and open her eyes. Their father had been a neglectful son of a bitch, and their mother, a whore.

"How can you say that?" Sarah had cried. "She was your mother!"

He told her that Tom Sr. was not his real father—that their mother had had an affair. "Do the math, you moron," he said. "It couldn't have been him. He was out to sea."

With that she understood why he had always called their father Tom instead of Dad. The doctors said he was crazy. A sociopath, they'd called him; he didn't realize the wrong he had done. In the courtroom, her brother had shown no emotion at all.

And even after he'd been convicted, he had shown no remorse. He told her during the visit that he had killed their mother because of her lack of loyalty to him, her son. Instead of standing up to Tom, she'd been about to abandon him at some school for whack-jobs. He blamed Tom for the idea, and said he deserved to die, too. There was no way they were taking him from his home.

Sarah was devastated. She had lost both her parents, and her only brother was severely deranged. She left the hospital that day after telling him she'd forgiven him, which he'd just laughed at, and never went back to visit again. She finished college that year, changed her last name, and moved to Connecticut, where she had attended graduate school. She was determined to try and forget the horrific things Thomas had done to her parents and move on with her life.

* * *

Since it was Sunday, Madi wasn't sure if she should call. The girl she'd met in Rockland had said her father rented and delivered kayaks, but on a Sunday? She decided to try the number, and sure enough, Jim Forrester answered.

He happened to be heading up to Camden that morning, and said he could drop off a kayak and life jacket on his way. He only had a two-person craft available, but she should be able to maneuver it just fine.

"I'll take it," she said.

She had been eyeing the island offshore since her arrival, and couldn't wait to get out on the water. After coffee on the patio, she dressed, applied sunblock, and loaded her waterproof camera, a protein bar, and a bottle of water into a backpack.

By the time Mr. Forrester delivered the bright yellow kayak, the tide was just starting to come in and the water was a bit choppy. He showed her how to adjust the foot pedals and gave her tips on the best body position for rowing. She was grateful when he offered to carry the kayak down to the edge of the rocks for her, then wondered if you were supposed to tip the kayak deliveryman like you would the pizza guy. When she tried, he simply smiled and said, "No, thank you, miss." After he informed Madi he would be back for the kayak on Saturday morning before she checked out, he departed and she headed toward the beach.

Madi dragged the kayak over the rocks, across the sand, and to the water's edge. To get in she would have to get wet—at least up to her shins. The water was absolutely freezing, and she wondered if it ever got warm enough to actually swim in. This was quite different from the Jersey Shore, where her family had vacationed every summer. She remembered a local joke she'd heard in Rockland: There are only two seasons in Maine—winter, and the Fourth of July. She gasped as the icy cold water touched her feet.

The island was southeast of the curving shore of Mahalas

Lane. It was hard to tell how far away it was, but it certainly seemed doable. She rowed south along the coast, past the beautiful homes on her right, built right up to the rocky cliff. *What views they must have,* she thought, and laid the paddle across her lap to take a few shots with her camera. Once she had passed about five houses, the coast got rockier and the trees denser. She couldn't see around the corner to the right yet, but imagined there would be more homes. The wind was pretty strong in her face and the boat rocked from side to side. The closer she got to the tip, the more lobster buoys she saw floating all around her. She wondered if lobsters came in with the tide.

The buoys were amazing to photograph, each one painted a different color. Many of them wore glowing neon shades, and stood out against the darkness of the water. It was apparent that each lobsterman had their own color scheme—purple and yellow, red and white, green and pink, solid blue, and so on. Apparently, this was how they identified their traps amid the sea of buoys. She imagined the sheer number of lobsters swimming in the dark sea beneath her.

When she reached the tip of the peninsula she saw a wooded inlet to her right that led to a single home on a large lawn, jutting out into the water. At the edge of the lawn, a small row of rocks lined a wide sandy beach. The house was a huge Maine gray shingle with a wraparound porch studded with rocking chairs. On the lawn, two whitewashed Adirondack chairs faced the unoccupied island that was Madi's final destination. The property and the home were spectacular.

She took some shots of the house and then put her camera away to concentrate on rowing out to the island on her left.

Without the trees of the peninsula blocking the wind, she was fighting the tide full force now. As each minute passed, she thought of how close it had seemed from the beach. Her arms began to ache, and she started to wonder if this had been a bad idea. No one knew she was out on the water, and as she glanced behind her, she questioned whether she could swim ashore if need be.

She was halfway there, so she might as well keep going, she thought. If she wasn't afraid to walk down the streets of New York alone, what was she so afraid of now? Capsizing? Drowning? Sharks? *All of the above!* She laughed aloud at herself.

As Madi finally neared the island, she realized it had taken more than a half-hour of intense rowing to get there. Definitely farther than she'd planned for her first leisurely kayak trip. As she approached the shore, she turned left to avoid the wind coming in from the right. She followed the coast around to the easternmost side of the island, maneuvering her way around more lobster buoys and large rocks that protruded above the surface. Most of the island was covered with pine trees. On the eastern tip was an inlet where she could pull the kayak ashore.

Madi landed on a beach that was made up of millions of pieces of crushed shells rather than sand, and pulled the kayak up far enough to ensure that it wouldn't float away. In front of her were some huge rock formations covered in live seaweed. Realizing how slippery the piles of seaweed were, she carefully made her way across the rocks, trying to get to the highest point. As she climbed the seagulls moved away in unison, screeching at her for disturbing their resting spot. She could hear a bell on the other side, warning boats not to get too close to the rocky coast, but she couldn't yet see it.

At the top, she collapsed onto a rock and caught her breath before shooting photos of the floating bell she could now see, rocking in the foggy sea air. She pulled out her water for a sip and gazed back at the peninsula. Her cottage and boathouse were long since out of sight. She laid back on the rock and breathed in the cool salt air, daydreaming about living on a deserted island like this. She imagined the house she had just seen on the peninsula being built here on this island, and sitting on a rocking chair next to the man of her dreams, watching the sunset together every evening. She pictured picnic tables where she would serve chowder and lobster to her family and friends who had come by boat to visit for long weekends. She could even imagine a little child running around the island, bringing her new shells to display in the kitchen window.

After about an hour of sunning herself, she grew hungry for more than the protein bar, which she had eaten on the ride out, so she slid her way down the rocks to the kayak and embarked on the long trip back to Mahalas Lane.

*   *   *

Madi had hardly enough strength to haul the yellow kayak up the rocks and over the slope to the pathway, dragging it one pull at a time while balancing on the piles of rocks. When she made it to the path, she slid the kayak along its side and nestled it amid the sea of purple wildflowers. Unzipping her life jacket, she grabbed the paddle and walked up to the boathouse, tossing the items on the floor and collapsing onto the bed.

The interior of the boathouse was like a basic one-room

cabin. While most boathouses were made to store boating and beach equipment, this one had clearly been built to provide additional accommodations. There was a makeshift kitchenette, a small built-in bed with a foam mattress, handmade bookshelves, and a tiny table with two old wooden chairs. Reflecting much of its original design, it was far more rustic than the nicely decorated, all-white interior of the cottage with its coastal-themed motif and charming bead-board walls. The recent addition of a deck and double French doors helped to enhance the primitive furnishings. *Maybe I'll sleep out here one night and enjoy the ocean breeze coming through the doors,* she thought.

By now it was almost two o'clock and she hadn't eaten a solid meal yet. She decided to make herself a sandwich and maybe take another nap. This time, however, she would curl up on the slip-covered sofa instead of the Adirondack chair she'd snoozed on yesterday, on the boathouse porch. She flashed back to Josh waking her from her catnap, and smiled. How long ago that suddenly seemed. If the days continued to feel this long, her trip would feel more like a month than a week. Exactly what the doctor ordered.

When she got back to the cottage, she saw an envelope stuck between the screen and the front doors. It was blank, and Madi assumed it was a note from the rental agent who had said she'd be stopping by sometime to welcome her. She grabbed it and walked inside, tearing it open as she kicked off her water shoes. She paused to hang her beach towel on one of the hooks by the door, then pulled out the folded notecard.

Inside was a hand-drawn coupon that featured a clumsy rendering of a lighthouse, which made Madi laugh, along with the words GOOD FOR ONE FREE NIGHT OF STARGAZING.

Along the bottom were additional instructions: REDEEM THIS OFFER AT THE OWLS HEAD LIGHT KEEPER'S COTTAGE ANY TIME AFTER 9 P.M. TONIGHT.

After a long shower, Madi sat down with her freshly made tuna sandwich and thought about Josh's handcrafted invitation. *This could be dangerous.* If Kristen were here, she would be all over this. There was nothing her friend wanted more these days than for Madi to find herself a man. Lingering over the note as she ate her lunch, she thought, *What's the harm of a little summer fun? No strings attached.*

CHAPTER SEVEN

It was another long day for Josh. To his knowledge, there had never been a murder in Owls Head. He was quickly learning that they create more paperwork than any other crime he had ever encountered. He had to go back down to Boothbay to complete his statement and then over to the state attorney's office. He also wanted to check on Bill Andrews's bond. Since the charge would be first-degree murder, the bond was likely to be more than the lobsterman could afford, but Josh still wanted to be certain Andrews wouldn't be released.

Josh's mother had called him first thing that morning as soon as she'd seen the paper. "Thank *God* you answered, Josh. Are you all right?" She sounded exasperated.

"Mom, I'm fine. Why?"

"You're in today's paper! It says you found a woman's dead body, and that it was murder!"

Josh sighed. His mother could be a little dramatic.

"It's in the paper?" he asked.

"Front page!" she exclaimed, like he'd won an Oscar.

"Mom, everything is okay. It was a domestic violence incident. The guy is in jail."

"The paper said you were alone when you found her. Was the killer there? Did he have a weapon?"

"Seriously, Mom, relax. I'm fine."

"Josh, your father would absolutely blame himself if anything happened to you. He wanted you to be an engineer, you know."

He quickly diverted her. "Listen, Mom, I've got another call. I'll have to talk to you later."

"Okay, call me back. I love you, sweetie, and I'm glad you're all right."

"Love you too, Ma," he said, and quickly hung up.

He could only imagine the unnecessary attention he'd get about this at the next town meeting. He could hardly wait.

As the evening turned to night, he glanced outside more than a few times, wondering if Madi had gotten his note yet. When nine o'clock came and went, then ten and eleven, he couldn't help but feel disappointed. And a bit embarrassed. He'd made a fool of himself, leaving the coupon.

Admittedly, Josh Daniels had never been a lady's man. He had very little experience at romancing women. In high school he'd been more focused on sports than girls; the handful of dates he'd been on had never amounted to anything. Later, at the law enforcement academy, the few women in his class had hardly given him a second glance.

While his mother was an avid matchmaker, trying to set Josh up with all her friends' daughters—or any pretty girl who walked into the museum, for that matter—it was difficult to meet single women in small-town Maine. Since Madi hadn't shown up, she obviously hadn't felt the same connection he'd experienced with her the night before.

After staring at the ceiling for what felt like an eternity, Josh finally drifted off to sleep.

* * *

2001

Sarah Wilson had taught elementary school for more than twenty years before she'd become a principal. After another dozen and a half at the helm of the oldest school in West Simsbury, Connecticut, she was ready to retire. She had thought about returning to the Maine coast over the years, but wasn't sure she could bring herself to be anywhere near Owls Head.

She had never married. Her students had consumed her life. She loved their innocence, especially the youngest of them who hadn't yet had the opportunity to turn into bad seeds.

When she received the Maine real estate magazine she had ordered in the mail, Sarah's whole life flashed in front of her when she got to page twelve. From the photographs, she recognized it immediately, but somehow she still couldn't believe her eyes. Could it be? Was that her family's cottage in Owls Head? Her heart skipped a beat. When she'd made the decision after her parents' death never to return to her childhood home, the property was abandoned, and subsequently, the deed turned over to the bank.

The listing said the home was being sold "as is." It looked like it hadn't been touched in the more than thirty years since she'd left Maine. It had been up for auction, but in its current condition had not sold. The words jumped off the page and burned like a hot poker in her heart: "Once a charming home built in the shape of a boat, this cottage could be lovingly restored by the right owner."

She looked at the address on the listing and found her proof:

5 MAHALAS LANE, OWLS HEAD, MAINE. It was indeed her childhood home. Oh my God.

Her eyes welled up with tears. It had been many years since she had allowed the pain of her family's past to seep into her heart. She was certain she had buried it deep enough to never resurface.

It was a few weeks before she could look at the listing again, and sure enough, when she called the realtor, it was still for sale. After much painful deliberation, she made an appointment to see it.

It was time to face her past.

* * *

It was surprisingly dark in the house when Madi opened her eyes. The air had gotten undeniably cooler, and she was shivering from the breeze that came in through the living-room windows. The kayak trip had wiped her out, and her afternoon nap had apparently lasted longer than she'd planned.

She groped her way to the kitchen and flipped on the light switch. The boat-style lanterns that hung over the front windows lit up the room, and she squinted her eyes to adjust to the light. Madi couldn't believe the clock said 10:15. Had she really slept for six hours?

She suddenly remembered the note from Josh. Should she call him and explain why she hadn't shown up? She felt like a total heel. She knew he went to work early; would he be asleep by now? She decided not to take the chance of waking him. She would call him in the morning.

Madi opened the fridge and grabbed the Chardonnay. How late would she be up now that she'd practically gotten an entire night's sleep? She poured a glass, grabbed a sweatshirt, and went out the door. It was so quiet out here. She hadn't noticed how quiet it was the night before, since she'd been busy talking with Josh. She sat at the table and gazed up at the stars. This was a far cry from the lights of Manhattan. She loved New York—it was in her blood—but somehow she felt very comfortable here in Maine.

She thought about what she might want to do the next day. The puffin tour, the Wyeth Center, and shopping in Camden were all on her must-do list. If she wasn't too sore in the morning from her kayak trip, she might take a bike ride to the general store for breakfast. She had noticed some little lanes along the route when she'd driven to the store on her first day. Like Mahalas Lane, they led to the ocean, and Madi wanted to see some of the other houses on Owls Head. A little exploration by bicycle would be fun.

As she sat sipping her wine, she heard a rustling across the lane.

"Hello?" she called out. She couldn't see anything moving in the wildflowers that bordered the beach path. In the darkness, she could barely make out the silhouette of the green wooden bench that sat in the clearing at the top of the sloping property.

She heard more movement, then the silence returned. *Must have been an animal.* She was heading inside anyway, since the bugs were back. *Maybe it was one of those giant mosquitoes, heading down to the beach for a stroll.*

* * *

"Good morning, Lynne," Josh said as he stepped into the general store. The bells on the door chimed when he pushed it open. As a kid, they had always reminded him of Christmas jingle bells.

"Good morning, Joshua," Lynne Hardy replied from the sunken kitchen. "How are you?"

Josh knew she would be there even before he saw her, as she had been every morning for the past seventeen years. Her husband Porter was the financial manager for the city of Rockland, and she ran the store along with her three school-age children, who helped out on a hit-or-miss basis.

"Fine—and you?" he replied.

"I'm great. I hear you're a big hero now," she said with a grin.

"Have you been talking to my mother again?" They both chuckled.

"What'll it be?"

"I'll have a single banana-nut pancake."

"On a Monday? You never eat pancakes during the week. What's wrong?" she peered up from behind the counter with motherly concern.

"Why does something have to be wrong? I'm just hungry is all," he replied, slightly more defensive than he had intended.

"Sure, Josh. Coming right up."

* * *

Madi took a right turn and relished the feeling of coasting down the first hill on South Shore Drive. Her body was definitely feeling the aftermath of the kayaking excursion. On both sides of the road she saw house after house with lobster traps piled up in the yards. Some piles had matching buoys hanging neatly on the sides of the stacked traps, while some were huge messy heaps. There were so many traps that they almost dwarfed the tiny houses. Clearly, this road was filled with hardworking people.

She took every right turn she could find, which didn't amount to many, and weaved in and around the winding lanes by the water. As she neared each lane's end, she noticed the increased size of the homes. The closer to the water, the larger the homes. *Business owners and retirees*, she thought. She passed a grandmother on a porch with her grandchild, trying to sit him down at a table outside. She waved back at the little girl who was coming up from the beach in her swimsuit and heading into another impressive house. She watched a man trim a row of fuchsia flowers on the side of a beautiful pale yellow mini mansion. The car in that driveway said Massachusetts. *Summer home.*

At the end of her self-guided tour, she turned back onto Owls Head's main road at the minuscule cemetery with the freshly painted white picket fence. To her left she passed a sign that said Owls Head Library. The building was so small, she stretched her neck to see if there was another behind it. Nope, that was the library. *Unbelievable. There's a Starbucks on my corner larger than this town's library.*

She pulled into the five-car gravel lot of the Owls Head General Store and leaned the bike against the building. It had white siding with hunter-green wooden shutters, and green-and-white-striped awnings over the windows. The door was situated in the center, and the window boxes flanking each side were filled with colorful flowers. To the right of the building, there was an ice machine set against a fence that had painted buoys hanging on it, obviously intended to hide the trash cans beyond it.

To the left of the store was another small building whose

first floor served as the post office, and the second, as the sheriff's department. Between the two buildings was a decent-size lawn with a couple of worn picnic tables along with a pair of freshly painted red Adirondack chairs. *Apparently these chairs are required in Maine,* she thought. Through the left window of the store, she could see two ladies sitting at a table, chatting over breakfast.

She opened the screen door and stepped inside. To her right sat the cash register on a small counter, and beyond that was the open kitchen. To her left was a room filled with beverage coolers, grocery shelves, and tables. And standing directly in front of her next to the coffee stand was none other than Sheriff Joshua Daniels.

"Hi, Josh!" She greeted him with a big smile.

He replied sheepishly, "Well, umm, hi, Madi . . . How are you?"

"I'm great! Just took a long bike ride, and I'm starving," Madi proclaimed.

"Tell your friend about my pancakes, Joshua," Lynne instructed as she handed him his plate-sized pancake.

"Wow," Madi said to Lynne. "That's the biggest pancake I've ever seen. It looks delicious."

"The best in Owls Head," the shop owner continued.

"The only in Owls Head," Josh joked back at Lynne. She smiled and hollered toward Madi as she descended back into the sunken kitchen. "Let me know what you're havin' when you're ready, honey."

Josh looked down at the floor, avoiding eye contact with Madi. He was admittedly stung by her no-show the night before.

"I'll have the same!" Madi called down to Lynne, and then

turned to Josh.

"May I join you?"

"Sure," he said, and hesitated, still avoiding eye contact.

"Listen, I was going to call you when I got back from breakfast to explain about last night," Madi said. "I had gone kayaking—"

"You don't have to explain," Josh said, embarrassed.

"No, really, I want to. I was so wiped out from kayaking that I fell asleep at four and didn't wake up until almost ten-thirty. I didn't want to wake you by calling too late."

He tilted his head and gazed at her, trying to discern whether she was just being nice.

"Honest. I would have loved to stargaze with you," Madi said.

Josh felt relieved that he hadn't made a complete fool of himself after all.

Madi got a coffee with her pancake, and they talked about her kayak trip as they walked outside to the picnic tables. While they ate, she learned about the island she had paddled to—Monroe Island. Josh had gone there to fish with his dad when he was a kid. Turns out they used to launch their canoe close to the huge house Madi had admired, and they had spent almost every Saturday out there.

They talked about each of the homes Madi had passed, the people who lived in them, the cemetery, and the library. Josh told her that the library had some books that contained the history of Owls Head, including the records of every resident that had ever lived in the town. The library had been there since 1927, and the property had been purchased for fifty dollars. The post office behind where they were sitting was originally an ice-cream parlor, where dances and socials were held on the second floor.

Madi couldn't believe there were still towns like this left in America. Then she thought of St. Patrick's in Chinatown, reminding herself that Manhattan had its own special history.

Madi noticed the way Lynne raised her eyebrow and smirked at Josh when she came out to clear their plates. *This really is a small town,* she thought. *I'd better be careful; people are watching.*

Madi promised Josh she'd visit the lighthouse that night, and smiled as she rode away. She had to admit, the fact that he had missed her visit the night before was quite charming. At breakfast, she was reminded of just how handsome the sheriff was, especially in his uniform. *And, those blue eyes . . .*

CHAPTER EIGHT

After Madi returned from the general store, she took a shower and then strolled down toward her beach. It was almost high tide, so the sand was completely gone and the water had risen a few feet up the rocky embankment. She navigated along the rocks, bending over to look closely at them. She began selecting a few of her favorites and putting the small ones in her pockets. She placed the larger ones on a huge rock for later transport to the cottage.

Madi had noticed the neat rows of carefully chosen rocks surrounding the gravel patio where she and Josh had had drinks the other night. She imagined all of the renters who had contributed to the Zen-like formation. She would add a couple of her favorites before the week was over, and leave her mark on the place. She particularly liked the sparkly ones, and the really flat ones. *They're like pancakes,* she thought, which made her think of Josh. *What am I getting myself into tonight?* she asked herself. *Just a casual walk to the top of a lighthouse with a new friend, or something more?* As she continued her search for the perfect rocks to add to the collection, her thoughts kept drifting back to Josh. She decided she would look for a few more and then head up to Camden to do a little shopping.

She heard the bark just seconds before she felt the dog's cold nose on the back of her leg. She gave a quick jump and spun around to see a golden retriever perching on the stones behind her. He greeted her with a bark and some frantic sniffing, his tail wagging like crazy.

"Well, hello there, fella," Madi said. She dropped the rocks she had just scooped into her hands and squatted down to his level. He licked her face and she scratched behind both ears.

"Where did you come from, big boy?" Madi continued. "Huh? Tell me, where?"

Her doggie talk made him wag even harder, and his whole body shook with excitement. He barked again and pulled on her shorts with his paw.

"What is it? What do you want?" she asked.

He barked some more and spun around on the rocks.

"You want a rock?"

Madi picked up a rock and threw it some feet away. "Go get it, boy."

The retriever ran to the rock, picked it up in his mouth, and brought it back to her. Dropping it at her feet, he barked again. After about fifteen minutes and countless fetches, Madi sat on the rocks for a rest, having grown tired of their game before the dog had. She wondered why no one had come to claim him.

"No more, buddy," she apologized. "That's enough for me. Time for you to go home." After she'd pet him a few more times, the dog finally retreated down the peninsula on the rocks and into the trees beyond. *He must live in one of those houses that jut out over the water,* she thought as she started back to the cottage.

When she pulled the screen door open to grab her purse, another envelope fell onto the ground. Smiling to herself, she ripped open Josh's latest letter.

* * *

"Are you kidding me?" Josh demanded furiously.

"No, sir, I'm not. He made bail," replied the clerk at the other end of the line.

"Fifty thousand dollars?" he asked in disbelief.

"Yes, sir."

"Well, did anyone follow him?"

"I don't know, sir."

Josh hung up angrily and put a call in to the Boothbay sheriff. He was in meetings, Josh was told. He left an urgent message.

I can't believe it, he thought. *Where did he get that kind of money?* Then he thought of the piles of cash on the bar. Bill had claimed he'd had a good catch. *A few hundred, maybe, but not fifty thousand.*

He headed over to Kay Andrews's place to make sure Bill hadn't been stupid enough to go back there to claim anything in the house. However, when he got there everything seemed to be in order.

He noticed that Madi's rental car wasn't in her driveway. *At least I'll get to see her later,* he thought.

* * *

Bill Andrews had been to the Black Bull to see Kay before. Everyone there knew he was Kay's ex, so they never acted overly welcoming. Tonight was no different. The barmaid Colleen stared at him coolly while he drank his first beer.

"What the hell are you lookin' at?" Bill scowled.

She turned away and tended to the other patrons. At her first opportunity, she would escape to the back and tell her manager he was here. They had been told he was in jail for killing Kay.

Bill watched the kitchen door open and close, waiting; he'd wait as long as it took for the man to leave out the back door to the employee lot. Then he would crush that piece of shit's head in, just like the guy had done to his Kay.

* * *

It was ten after nine when Josh saw headlights coming down the long road leading to the lighthouse.

"Hi there," Madi said when he opened the door.

"Hi yourself. Come on in."

From the outside, the house was of typical Maine style, with white siding and a red shingle roof. The inside, however, was like a museum, with photos of the keeper's house, the light, and the park dating back to the early 1800s. Beneath each frame hung a brass plaque with the date and description of the image. There were even portraits of every keeper's family.

"It's a little impersonal, I know," Josh said as he watched her move from photo to photo.

"These are amazing," Madi replied.

"Would you like a glass of wine?" he asked as he opened the fridge.

"I'd love one."

He poured them each a glass and showed her around the rest of the house. He skipped over his bedroom, since he hadn't made the bed. In the second bedroom, he showed her some artifacts from the lighthouse—pieces of equipment that had been replaced over the years, including one of the original lenses.

"The rest is at the Maine Lighthouse Museum in Rockland," Josh told her.

"Oh, yeah, I saw that place by the harbor. I haven't been to it yet."

After the house tour, Josh said, "It's pretty clear out tonight, so we should be able to see the stars really well. Are you ready to head up?"

"Sure," Madi said, and they stepped out into the cool night.

When they reached the base of the hill, Madi looked up to the lighthouse and remarked, "That's a lot of stairs."

"Forty-seven to be exact," he told her with a chuckle.

They walked around the top of the light and gazed out to the sea in every direction. The sliver of moon was just enough to barely make out the gentle rhythm of the water below. The sky was lit up like the Fourth of July, with millions of stars. They leaned against the tower and gazed upward in silence for quite some time.

"What made you come to Owls Head, Madi?" Josh said, breaking the silence.

"I was looking for a charming New England town, and found the cottage online."

"Do you always go on vacation alone to towns you've never been to?" he inquired.

"Actually, no; I usually go away with friends," she said a

bit defensively.

"But this time?"

"This time I wanted solitude—away from people, the city, my job."

"And here you are, spending all your time with me," he said, realizing he had monopolized a big part of her trip.

She turned to him. "No, really, it's okay. I'm enjoying this immensely. This is nothing like Manhattan, and you're nothing like the men there."

"I hope that's a good thing," he said, searching her eyes.

"It's a very good thing," Madi told him, and she could feel her heart beating in her chest as she looked up at him. It had been a while since Madi had had a man show this kind of interest in her, especially a sweet man like Josh. In the city, she was always either working or hanging out with colleagues after hours.

They held each other's gaze until Madi gave a shudder.

"You're cold," Josh said. "Here." He pulled his sheriff's department windbreaker off and swung it around Madi's back, resting his hands on her shoulders. He looked at her in the moonlight and felt himself shiver—but not from the temperature. It was most certainly something else. This woman had mesmerized him.

His hands moved from her shoulders and cupped her face, stroking her bottom lip with his thumb. She closed her eyes for a moment. When she opened them, he was moving toward her and she leaned in to meet him. He kissed her while pulling her closer, and the only sound she could hear was the heavy breathing between them. They kissed more and more intensely, and she wrapped her arms around him. She could feel every ripple and muscle in his back. He was in incredible shape.

She felt something building inside her, deep beneath her abdomen.

Josh slowly pulled away and looked at her face. He smiled, and Madi returned the smile. He had the softest lips and the gentlest hands she had ever felt. He was so large, yet so unassuming. They looked into each other's eyes for what seemed like an eternity.

"Where have you been all my life, Miss Madi Lyons?" he asked with a sigh. He was beyond smitten.

"New York," she replied with a smile.

* * *

Josh led her into his bedroom. He caressed her skin, as smooth as rose petals. She was the most beautiful woman he had ever seen, and he wanted to please her. He explored her body with his fingers and mouth, and she responded with little moans that lit a fire inside him. She stroked him rhythmically and he was aroused beyond belief, but did not want to rush it. He wanted this moment to last.

When she pulled him on top, she was pleading for him to enter her. He stared deep into her hazel-brown eyes and the world simply fell away. It was the most incredible lovemaking he had ever experienced. She was so warm inside he wanted to stay there forever, but he knew he was going to explode very soon, and they rocked together until they both let go. He collapsed on her and they held each other tight.

Wrapped in his muscular arms, Madi felt like a tiny star in a vast sky. He was strong, yet gentle as an ocean breeze. She'd never had an orgasm that intense, nor had she ever felt so much caring from a man. His generosity was abundant.

He clearly wanted to please her, and please her he had. She hoped she had done the same for him.

They lay there for some time, catching their breath before either spoke.

"I'm starving," Madi finally said.

"Me, too," Josh said, instantly leaping off the bed. She watched his firm white derriere disappear out the door. She laughed when he returned, still totally in the buff, carrying plates of sandwiches and chips, and under his arm, two beers.

She looked at her plate as she sat up, pulling the covers up over her chest.

"PB&J?" she asked in surprise.

"Specialty of the house," he replied as he bowed like a performer.

Madi had no idea what time it was, but they stayed up for hours, talking, kissing, making love, and holding each other.

When he asked about her family, Madi told him about her father's illness, and how her family had coped with it since her childhood. She shared stories about visits to hospitals, and even his death a few years ago. She was surprised at how easy it was to open up with him, something she rarely did with anyone other than Kristen.

He asked more questions about her career, and she told him that she had known she wanted to be in advertising since she was a kid. She had a natural talent for art, and as a young teen, was accepted into a summer art program that convinced her to become a graphic designer. Madi explained that she had left home at seventeen for college and had never lived with her parents again. She was overtly independent and couldn't wait to get out on her own. Determined to succeed, she confessed to him that she had even changed her name for the betterment of her career.

"Your real name isn't Madi?"

"No, my first name *is* Madelyn, but I modified my last name."

"From?"

"It was DeLeone, and I changed it to Lyons so it wouldn't sound so Italian. I know it sounds silly, but advertising is still a bit of a man's world, and I wanted to do anything I could to be taken seriously."

He laughed so hard that she started to take offense. When he saw her reaction, he pulled her close and rolled her around on the bed playfully. "You crazy, determined woman!" Josh tickled her.

"I just needed to not be the typical Italian New Yorker, that's all," she said.

"I think that's awesome—just like you."

Madi was touched by his sincerity. He was perhaps the nicest person she had ever met. And, one amazing and generous lover.

They made love again before they fell asleep, huddled together under his down comforter like two kittens.

Chapter Nine

Madi was alone in Josh's bed the next morning. A smile automatically spread across her face, recalling the night she'd spent with him. Stretching sleepily, she sat up and called out his name. When she got no response, she tiptoed out to the living room to see if he had gotten up during the night and fallen back to sleep on the sofa. Instead, she found one of Josh's notes on the kitchen table: "*Had to go to work. Last night was incredible. Call you later—Josh.*"

She smiled and put his note in her purse, which lay on the sofa. She remembered she had forgotten to ask him about the meaning of his note from the day before. She was still puzzled by what he had written. He had simply said, "It's mine."

She got dressed and let herself out, quickly jumping in her car when she saw the tourists passing by on their way to the lighthouse. The clock in the rental car said it was 9:30 a.m., and as she drove the mile-long road to exit the park, she saw dozens of people already scattered along the way, taking photos of sailboats.

Back at her cottage, she climbed the stairs to the second floor and walked through the series of three loft-style bedrooms connected by doorways without doors. She had only been up here once since she'd arrived, choosing to stay in the main-floor bedroom instead. This morning, the claw-foot tub in the second-floor bathroom was calling her name, and she settled in for a long soak.

Her mind replayed every delicious detail of her night with Josh. He had looked so deeply and intently at her, she was convinced he was looking right into her soul. He made her feel extremely safe when she was with him.

Am I falling for this guy? Madi asked herself.

Madi knew she'd hardened her exterior for self-protection, the way she had prepared for her father's death. She didn't want to get hurt. She wasn't ready for anything real. At the same time, she had never felt so free to be herself around a man.

She heard the creaking of the screen door and the click of the latch. Whoever it was knew the door had a tendency to slam shut, and held it carefully. *Must be Josh,* she thought, and called down to him.

"I'm up here," she hollered, "taking a bath."

She could hear the creak of the wooden floor below as the person moved across the room. *Josh must be doing some follow-up on the case next door,* she thought. Maybe she could coax him out of that scratchy polyester uniform.

"Josh, come join me," she invited.

The door closed quietly, the same way it had opened, and the house became silent again.

Oh my God—it must have been the rental agent! Madi thought, horrified. And she had yelled out *Come join me* . . . How embarrassing!

Madi quickly dried off and ran down the stairs in her towel to the bedroom, scurrying to find clothes. Quickly dressing, she rushed out the front door, looking around for the agent, but saw no one. No car, either. She giggled to herself. *What must she have thought?* Madi had told her she was vacationing alone.

It took her a couple minutes to locate Freda Smythe's phone number, and, not surprisingly, Madi got her voicemail. She left her a message to call when she got a chance, even though she didn't really expect to hear back from her after what had just happened.

* * *

Josh had gotten the call at ten after six that morning, just a few hours after they had fallen asleep. Madi had hardly stirred, and he was careful not to wake her as he silently got dressed. His dispatcher had received a call from a Rockland resident who had found the body of a man in his late thirties shortly before six a.m. The caller had been walking his dog along Limerock Street, and when he'd neared the corner of Limerock and Main, his dog had pulled him toward a pile of trash near the dumpster at the rear of the Black Bull Tavern. When the dog's owner realized it wasn't trash but a dead body, he had called 9-1-1.

The victim was Robert Peterson, line cook at the Tavern. He had ended his shift at 11 p.m., and after enjoying a couple of beers with his coworkers, had headed out the rear door to his car. He must have been struck from the back, as half of his skull was crushed in.

Josh was able to reach manager Ron Elliot, who'd been on duty the night before, and arranged for him to come to the station for an interview. Elliot informed Josh that Bill Andrews had been to the bar the night before; he had told Bill to leave the premises and not return, and hadn't seen him for the rest of the shift. The manager said he knew there had been something going on between Kay and the cook, but he didn't believe it was anything serious.

The man was rightfully concerned that two of his employees had now been brutally murdered, and Josh agreed to speak to the Rockland sheriff's office about adding more patrols to the neighborhood surrounding the Tavern. Josh reassured him that it was his top priority to bring Andrews in for questioning in this latest killing, and to arrest him if the evidence was sufficient.

Josh was convinced that Andrews had committed both crimes. He'd wanted vengeance on his ex-wife, killing her first, and now, he'd killed her boyfriend. He suspected Andrews had finished what he had come to do and wouldn't be returning to the Tavern anytime soon. Now they just had to find him.

* * *

Madi was exhausted from the past couple of days. She decided the kayaking and biking had been a little too ambitious, and last night she'd stayed up way too late, so today she would just relax by the shore. She hadn't picked up her book in a while, so she grabbed a muffin and headed for the boathouse porch. She was reading Hemingway's *The Sun Also Rises*, the famous story of flamboyant Jake Barnes and his writer friends who travel to Spain for the running of the bulls. She found the writing spare yet powerful, and was impressed with the characters' ability to drink, eat, drink, eat, and then drink some more.

Madi was just getting to the part where the main character's love interest hooks up with the bullfighter when she heard a noise. A man dressed in a wet suit had appeared on a pathway to her right, heading toward the beach. Until that moment, she hadn't realized there was an adjacent beach path on that side of the cottage property. Startled by his sudden appearance, she let out a small squeal.

"I didn't know there was a path there," she explained when he stopped and looked over at her.

"So you're renting the Walker place?" the man asked.

"Yes, I am," she replied.

"Where are you visiting from?"

"Manhattan."

"Nice. How long are you staying?"

"A week," Madi said, then added, "The water seems way too cold for a swim."

"I'm used to it," he said.

"Do you live around here?" she asked.

"Up the way."

"On this street?" Madi asked.

"I grew up on this street," he replied.

"It's such a beautiful lane. Which house is yours—the white one, or the one with gray siding?"

"The brown one," he responded.

"I don't remember seeing a brown one," Madi said, trying to picture it.

"It's set back from the road—you can't really see it," he said. "Enjoy your vacation."

"And you enjoy your swim."

Madi returned to her reading, glancing up occasionally to gaze toward the water. By noon, the temperature outside was perfect—somewhere around 75 degrees. After another hour, she noticed the man hadn't yet returned from his swim. She decided to take a break and head down to the rocks to gather her loot from the other day.

When she got there, she looked around the bay for the swimmer but didn't see him anywhere. *He must have left the beach from a different path,* she thought. Just as she piled the last of her rocks onto the rotting picnic table at the crest of the path, she saw the familiar golden retriever. He was just standing there on the rocks, looking out to the sea. *Perhaps he belongs to the swimmer,* Madi thought as she returned to her perch on the deck.

* * *

The man had swum south and climbed out on the rocks between the cottage and the next house on the lane. He waited until she'd turned to put her book down and then snuck around the building. Later, he watched her stand up and head down to the edge of the rocks. She looked out at the water and then began carrying rocks to the table nestled in the wildflowers. He pulled back into the brush, waiting for her to make her way back to the cottage.

When she finally walked back up the path, he circled the boathouse behind her, preparing to surprise her from behind.

"Madi!" hollered a voice from the road.

"Hey, you!" she happily exclaimed.

Someone was up there. Perhaps the same someone she had called out for in the cottage earlier. He disappeared into the woods.

Madi jogged up to the top of the lawn and smiled crookedly at Josh.

"Hi there, Mr. Lighthouse."

"Hi there, Miss DeLeone."

"Oh God, don't call me that!" she said, giving him a little push.

He stepped very close to her and looked down into her eyes. "What are you going to do about it?" he asked, with the most horrible New York accent she had ever heard.

"I'll show you what I'm gonna do 'bout it!" she returned the exaggerated accent, fake-punching him in the chest.

"You know what I think?" his teasing continued.

"What, big man?" she said, jumping around like a boxer.

"I think you are full of baloney, Miss Day-Lee-Oh-Nee," he said, emphasizing every syllable.

"Oh yeah?"

"Yeah!" he said, and scooped her up like a rag doll, throwing her over his shoulder. With seemingly no effort, he carried her across the street and into the cottage.

"Now behave, Miss DeLeone, or I'm going to have to lock you up!" he said, dropping her onto the sofa.

"Promises, promises," she whispered, as he leaned over and began to kiss her.

After a few minutes of passionate kissing, he tore himself away and said he wasn't done working; he still had a few hours on duty. He would be back later that evening, and he'd bring dinner.

She asked if it was going to be peanut butter and jelly, and he replied, "Very funny." Then he winked, gave her another quick kiss, and was gone out the door.

Wow, this guy is really something, Madi thought as she watched him depart.

Chapter Ten

Madi was at the general store later that afternoon, looking at the small selection of wine, deciding she would choose one from the shelf labeled ORGANIC.

"It's Madi, isn't it?" a voice said.

She turned to see the owner of the general store behind her.

"Yes! Hello again, Lynne. How are you?"

"I'm well, thank you. May I help you with something?"

"I was thinking of trying one of these organic wines you have."

"What are you having it with?" she asked.

"Umm, I don't know exactly. My friend is bringing me dinner." Madi hesitated to say Josh's name, assuming that news traveled fast around here.

Lynne tilted her head and with a squint of her eyes, she pulled a bottle of Pinot Noir off the shelf.

"Aren't you staying at the old Walker cottage?" she asked.

"Yes, I am." *But you knew that already, didn't you, Lynne?*

"I love that house. It's always been one of my favorites on

Owls Head."

"Yes, it's so unique. Do you know anything about who built it?" Madi asked.

"Legend has it that a seaman built it for his new bride in the 1940s before he went out to sea. Unfortunately, they moved away in the fifties, and the house fell into disarray for a long time. I grew up in South Thomaston, so I don't know much else. One of the more recent owners fixed it up some, but it's the latest owner who has really put a lot of effort into it."

"It's been beautifully restored," Madi said.

"I've heard," Lynne said, handing Madi the bottle. "This is my favorite for a romantic dinner."

Oh geez . . . I knew I should've gone into town. She'd have to warn Josh, since he'd told Madi that Lynne was an old family friend.

"Thanks—I'll take it."

As she drove away from the two-building town center, she saw the sign for the library. She had a couple of hours to kill, as Josh wouldn't be over until at least five. She entered the small building and looked around the single room, which couldn't have been more than eight by ten feet—no larger than the living room of her New York City apartment. The wooden shelves surrounding her were filled with books, journals, periodicals, and charts.

After scanning the shelves for a few minutes, she settled on a long row of books labeled OWLS HEAD PROPERTY OWNERS. There were almost two dozen volumes, each about three inches thick. The dates on the spines began in the early 1800s and went all the way up to the current year. Hard to believe a town could have information on all of their residents compiled on a shelf barely longer than her body. With their gold foil trim, they reminded her of the old Encyclopedia Britannica set her parents had had in their house when she was growing up.

She scanned through the years until she found the one for 1940–49. She sat on one of two country benches arranged back-to-back in the center of the room. On the small circular table next to the benches stood a wooden statue of an owl wearing a pair of reading glasses. *The iconic symbol of wisdom,* she thought, aptly befitting, given the town's name.

She flipped through the handwritten pages, arranged by date. It took a long time to find it, but toward the back of the book, there it was: 5 Mahalas Lane. Owners: Thomas and Margaret Walker. Year built: 1942. Another entry had been made in the following year—Child born: Sarah Ann Walker, 1943. Further down after the taxes and property measurements, another entry. Child born: Thomas Phillip Walker, Jr., 1947.

Lynne had told her the family had moved in the 1960s, so Madi returned the book to the shelf and pulled out the one from two decades later. She spent some time skimming through the pages, but before she could find anything, the rear door to the library opened.

"Good afternoon," an older lady said softly.

"Hello," Madi said, standing up.

"Can I help you?" the woman asked, glancing at the book Madi had placed on the bench.

"I'm visiting Owls Head and thought I might look for a book to read," Madi answered.

The librarian pointed to the large volume. "I'm afraid those books cannot be checked out."

"Oh no, I was just looking up information about the house

I'm staying in. I thought the history would be interesting."

"Which house is it?" she asked.

Madi found it amusing that people in Owls Head seemed to know every single house in town. She was barely able to describe the buildings on the other side of her block, let alone a whole town—although in a place this size, she wasn't entirely surprised.

"Five Mahalas Lane."

"Ah, the old Walker place."

"That's what I've been told."

"Well, that home was built by Thomas Walker for his bride Margaret in 1942, as a gift to her. He was out to sea when their first child was born. They lived in the cottage for about twenty years."

Madi thought of the wooden bench situated at the top of the sloping path to the beach, and remembered the words carved on the back: MAGGIE'S BENCH. When she had first sat on the bench, she was struck by the perfect view of the bay beyond the boathouse. Margaret must have sat there for hours, looking out to sea, waiting for her husband to return. *How romantic and yet how sad,* Madi thought. And to have given birth to her child alone, without her husband by her side . . . it seemed like such a lonely life.

"Where did they go?"

"Their forwarding address is unknown."

"And after them?"

"The house was empty for a long period. Those were rough times in Owls Head. The house was bought and sold a number of times after they left, but none of the owners did the required maintenance necessary for the cold winters up here. A bank in Camden finally seized the house, and it went to auction in the early seventies, with no success. Rumors had spread that the bank wanted to build condos on the property and the adjacent parcels. The town wouldn't allow it, so it sat empty until the nineties."

"Who bought it then?"

"A nice lady named Sarah Wilson, from Connecticut. She came here to retire. She fixed it up some, and lived there until last year, when she passed away."

"What happened to her?"

"She took a terrible fall down the steps and hit her head on the brick fireplace at the bottom of the stairs."

"That's just awful," Madi gasped, picturing the exact location.

"Such a shame," the librarian agreed. Then, after a moment, she said, "The woman who bought the place after Sarah passed really did a fine job. Some of the older residents say it's nearly like it was when it was first built."

"Yes, it's very nice," Madi said distantly. She was saddened by Sarah's story.

The librarian turned to the wall nearest the door. "Here's our fiction section; I'm sure you can find a good read over here. When you're ready, just sign the book out on the clipboard behind the door. Have a nice day, dear."

With that, the lady said good-bye and left through the same door she had entered. Madi placed the heavy volume in its proper spot and left without signing anything out. She had lost interest after hearing the sorrowful tale of the late Sarah Wilson.

* * *

Bill knew he couldn't go back to the Lobster Dock ever again, but he really needed a drink. He would leave Maine soon, once he'd tied up some loose ends. There were some people who owed him money, and he wasn't going to let them off scot-free. He also had one more stop in Owls Head, to collect some of the items that Kay had taken in their divorce.

After shaving his beard and throwing on a baseball cap and glasses so he wouldn't be recognized, he found a bar in Tenants Harbor he would belly up to until dark. While he sipped on his favorite scotch, he thought about Kay. As much as he hated to admit it, he had truly loved her.

* * *

Madi was in her bedroom when she heard Josh arrive just after five o'clock. She twisted her clean, wet hair up into a clip and headed for the kitchen.

Josh was standing outside one of the front windows, grinning.

"May I help you, sir?" she asked in her most polite voice.

"I'll take a hot dog, fries, and a cotton candy, please."

"Coming right up!"

Josh had observed earlier that the windows on the front of the cottage resembled a concession stand at a fair. Unfortunately, the screens didn't open, so she couldn't pretend to pass the imaginary items through. Instead, she went outside, letting the door slam behind her, eager to greet him. He dropped the bags he was carrying and hugged her.

"How was your day?" she asked.

"Very long without you," Josh said, "and stressful. But much better now that I'm here."

She rewarded him with a lingering kiss. Then she looked down at his bags.

"What have we here, Sheriff?"

"A taste of Maine," he announced proudly.

"What is it?"

"Fresh steamed lobsters from Jesse's Market—the best in all of Knox County," he bragged.

"My mouth is watering!" she replied. "I'll set the table."

"Do you have a grill?" he asked.

"I think so—in the barn."

"I'll check," he said, and headed out back.

Madi brought out the bottle of red wine from the general store, two glasses, and a pile of dishes, bowls, and utensils. Josh had returned with a small charcoal grill, and set up a station for himself on the stone patio. Out of his car came a bag of charcoal, along with ears of corn and a head of fresh broccoli he had picked up at the farmers' market in Rockland. He lit the charcoal, wrapped the veggies in foil, placed them on the grill, and took a seat beside Madi.

They sipped their wine and gazed out at the ocean across the lane, enjoying the view and each other's presence. After a comfortable silence, Josh asked Madi how she had spent her day.

"I relaxed by the beach and read for a while," she told him. "You wore me out last night."

He blushed.

"Oh, and I met a guy who lives up the road."

"A guy?"

"Easy, boy—he's like fifty-something."

"From up the road?" Josh asked curiously. His questioning made Madi uncomfortable.

"Look, I'm not sure what your issue is; I was just talking to him." Madi was not one to beat around the bush. She wasn't going to have a man question her, especially on a second date.

"What did he look like?" Josh continued his interrogation.

"Josh, what is your problem?" she stood up, ready for battle.

"Madi, there is nobody that lives on this road that fits that description. I need to know what he looked like," he said. He stood up to face her, and continued. "I need to know; this is serious."

"What do you mean?" she said, backing down.

"I'll explain in a minute. First, tell me exactly what happened," he insisted.

She relayed the conversation with the man in the wet suit, describing him as mid- to late fifties, about six feet tall. He was wearing a swim cap and mask, but she thought she saw a little gray hair sticking out.

Josh told her about the man who'd been found dead in Rockland, and the fact that Bill Andrews had made bail and was a possible suspect in this second murder. He didn't want to worry her, but the description she'd just given matched that of Andrews.

After Josh called in her story to Dispatch, he did his best to focus on Madi. He had every deputy on his force out on patrol, looking for Andrews. They knew to call him immediately with any updates.

"Why would he come back here?" she asked, concerned. "And why would he just walk up and talk to me like that if he knew the cops were looking for him?"

"I don't know; it doesn't make sense. I just want you to be safe."

"Me, too." she said, moving closer to him. "I'd feel safer if you stayed here with me tonight."

"You don't have to ask twice," he assured her, wrapping his arms around her waist.

"Thanks, Josh," she said, leaning in to kiss him.

"The corn is burning," Josh mumbled as they continued to kiss. They were standing in front of the cottage, arms around each other, making out like teenagers.

Despite his wandering thoughts about the case, dinner was wonderful. They had donned the plastic bibs that came with the meal, and he walked Madi through the art of taking apart an entire lobster—first, ripping off the claws, and then gripping the body and pulling it inside out. He showed her how to get the meat out of each part of the lobster, so as not to miss a single tasty morsel.

He laughed as she made a mess, squirting lobster juice all over. The lobster tail was sweeter than any Madi had ever tasted in a restaurant, and the warm salty butter was like the cherry on a sundae.

Everything was scrumptious, even the charcoal-encrusted corn, which he had left on a bit too long. It didn't matter. He was just happy to be there with her.

* * *

Madi was nuzzled into his chest, half asleep as he nibbled on her neck.

"Not again, Josh—I'm tired."

"I can't get enough of you, Madelyn DeLeone," he whispered in her ear.

"Aren't you exhausted? You got up so early."

He coaxed her with his lips, kissing her neck, then her right breast, and down to her belly. She began to shift around under the covers and moaned softly, a hint that there was still a chance she could be persuaded. As he lifted his head up toward her face to kiss her, he caught a flash of light out of the corner of his eye and froze.

"What's wrong?" Madi asked.

"I saw a light," he said, staring out the bedroom window toward Kay Andrews's A-frame. A moment later: "There it is again."

Josh was off the bed in a split second, pulling his pants on and grabbing his shirt and shoes as he ran out of the room.

"Josh!" she called after him.

"Lock the door behind me," he instructed.

She heard him go into the barn where he had parked his squad car for the night.

Small town, he'd explained. *No explanation necessary,* she had replied.

He's getting his gun, she thought. She locked the door and went back to the bedroom.

She looked out the window where Josh had first noticed the light and saw what appeared to be a flashlight moving through the darkness. *Was it outside, or in the house next door?* Terrified at the thought of the murderer roaming around outside her cottage, she moved from the bedroom and stepped into the hallway, away from any glass.

She was standing by the staircase, facing the edge of the wall with the fireplace in the living room. *This must be where Sarah Wilson met her fate.* Madi's skin began to tingle. This cottage was suddenly becoming a lot less charming.

Where was Josh?

She thought she heard footsteps outside, running past the cottage, then Josh yelling something. The noise got farther away, until nothing.

She took a couple steps through the living room in the dark, grateful that the lights in the cottage were out. No one could see her there. As she approached the front windows, which were still hanging open on the hooks, she stopped dead in her tracks.

There he was, looking at her through the screened window.

She screamed as loud as she could. "Josh, Josh—he's here!" she screeched as she ran upstairs. "Josh!"

She crouched in the bathroom of the back bedroom, behind the only door on the second floor, frozen with fear for what seemed an eternity. In the distance, she thought she heard a dog barking. *Where was Josh?!*

"Madi!" She eventually heard him banging on the door downstairs. "Let me in!"

She cautiously came out of the bathroom and bent down to look out the octagonal window near the floor of the bedroom wall. She saw the flashing lights of a police car parked in the road, and she knew it wasn't Josh's. There were other officers there as well. She descended the stairs and let Josh in.

"I saw him, through the window. He looked right at me." She pointed to the front of the cottage.

"It's okay—he's gone." Josh stroked her hair as she shivered in his arms.

"You didn't catch him?"

"No, but believe me, Andrews is not coming back here tonight. He knows we'll be waiting for him."

CHAPTER ELEVEN

The cottage was bright and sunny the next morning when Josh tiptoed out of the bedroom. It had been late when Madi finally fell asleep, and he didn't want to wake her just yet.

He found the coffee and filters and started a pot. Sitting in a damp patio chair outside, he replayed the events of the previous night. It was a lot to digest. The fact was, he had become intimately involved with a tourist, and last night he had put her in danger by chasing a murderer while leaving her alone. There was one problem: Madi wasn't just a tourist to him. He cared for her, and he wasn't going to leave her vulnerable again.

Today, he would make it up to her. His deputies and the adjacent county authorities were searching for Andrews up and down the coast, and Josh would be called in when he was located and taken into custody.

Back inside the cottage, he poured himself a cup of coffee and sat down on the sofa. As he placed his feet on the coffee table, he knocked over some papers. Picking them up from the floral area rug, he recognized his own writing on the top notecard. Smiling, he read the two notes he had written to Madi over the past couple of days. There was a third note in the pile, but the writing wasn't his. Josh read it over and over. *What an odd message.*

Leaving the note on the table, he went upstairs to wake Madi.

"Good morning, sunshine," Josh whispered as he planted a soft kiss on Madi's cheek.

"Hmm," she moaned, stirring a bit.

"Rise and shine," he said. "Your kayak awaits."

Madi stretched and smiled, sitting up as Josh handed her a mug of coffee. "My kayak?"

"Yup. We're going on an adventure."

* * *

The damn dog was barking again. He had only himself to blame, as he was the one who had trained the dog to warn him of trespassers. While the camp was far back in the woods, sometimes more adventurous tourists decided to explore beyond the beaches and rocks of the island's perimeter.

As soon as he heard the dog's first bark, he would typically lock him in his cage and quiet him with discipline. The muzzle hung right next to the leather whip on the wall should the dumb-ass decide to disobey. Fortunately, this time the dog stopped barking, so he didn't have to go outside and bring him in.

Lying on his bunk, he stared above him at the photos pasted to the ceiling. A single picture of his mother and sister gazed pathetically back at him, next to a photo of his childhood home—daily reminders of both the immorality of women and his rightful ownership of the cottage and boathouse.

He felt the familiar heat of anger rising in his chest and up to his ears. It was a feeling they had been able to control by forcing him to take his meds—but the days of numbness were over. He was himself again. Angry. Bitter. Scornful. He would have his final revenge on all of them soon.

But in the meantime, he calmed himself by replaying the glorious moments when he'd stripped the life out of each of his victims.

* * *

Josh and Madi made a decent picnic from the limited selection in her fridge. They gathered the bottle of wine they hadn't finished the night before, plastic cups, grapes, apples, and a block of cheese from the general store. Madi diced the cheese and placed it with the fruit in Ziploc bags, packing it all into the backpack.

Once in the kayak, they propped their water bottles between their legs and started to row. Josh called out orders like a drill sergeant from the front seat—left, right, left, right— until Madi splashed him using her paddle. She couldn't believe he'd talked her into a repeat ride to Monroe Island, especially since she was still a bit sore from Monday.

"C'mon, Madi, I've been dying to go there since you told me about your trip," he said. "I haven't been out there in so long."

"All right already," she said with a wink.

It was amazing how different it was, paddling against the

tide with a man like Josh in the kayak. *I like seeing him like this,* she thought as she watched the muscles in his back ripple from side to side.

"Are you sure you're paddling back there?" he kept asking. Whenever he turned his head she would start rowing. He eventually caught on to her antics.

"You think you're funny, DeLeone."

"I know I am, Daniels."

On the left turn toward the beach, Madi spotted a deer in the woods to her right.

"Did you see that?" she asked excitedly. There weren't too many deer running around Manhattan—only miniature plastic ones named Rudolph in apartment windows, or on gigantic floats in the Macy's Thanksgiving Day Parade.

Josh had seen the movement, but didn't catch sight of the deer.

They pulled the kayak up on the same beach that Madi had visited, and left their life jackets in the seats. They climbed only far enough onto the rocks to find a flat one to sit on that had no seaweed. They toasted to having met each other, and the good time they'd had this week, despite the circumstances. Looming in the back of both their minds was Madi's impending departure, and crazy Bill Andrews. But for now they would focus on each other.

Josh leaned on his right elbow and fed Madi grapes with his left hand. He kissed the wine off her lips and tasted the saltiness on her neck. She giggled and kissed him back. Josh's crystal blue eyes intoxicated Madi; while he was large in stature, she adored the baby face that matched his round smiling eyes. With his English heritage, his features were completely the opposite of Madi's, who had a slender, angular face and Mediterranean complexion.

The breeze was blowing lightly and the bell in the distance blended with the sound of the waves hitting the rocks. The birds called out as Josh and Madi began exploring each other.

Madi felt like she was in one of her dreams. Her head told her not to take this thing with Josh too seriously, but her heart was undoubtedly feeling something more. She sat up on the rock and pulled her shirt off, feeling the salt air on her breasts. Madi felt free on this little island in the middle of the ocean— free to lose her inhibitions. She climbed on top of Josh and pushed his chest backward on the rock. He was aroused, and before long, their shorts were off and she was arching her back while she rocked with him beneath her, inside her. Their soft moans grew deeper and huskier with each thrust. He held her hips and moved her back and forth with the sound of the cresting waves. He couldn't resist this woman.

"Oh my God!" Madi cried out as she felt the world rushing in around her.

Josh sat up and pulled her tightly toward him, while he joined her in a united orgasm. He grabbed her face and kissed her, whispering, "You are so beautiful, Madi—so beautiful."

What was happening between them? Madi thought, overwhelmed.

* * *

He had seen many lovebirds come to the island over the years. They only came for one reason: to satisfy their sexual desires. When he arrived at the crest above the eastern beach, he saw them on the rocks out by the bell. *Another whore*, he snarled, and retreated into the woods to prepare for his ride to the mainland. He exited the woods on the southwestern side, down the concealed path to his kayak, which was hidden from view. No tourist ever came ashore here, as the coast on this side had no beach.

Today, he would claim what was rightfully his.

* * *

"Want to explore the island?" Madi asked while they stared at the clouds above.

"Are you serious?"

"Yeah, c'mon—you said this was going to be an adventure."

"Madi, it's very rocky and overgrown up there, and you don't have the right shoes for hiking."

"C'mon, Josh, please?" she begged.

"You're very persistent, you know that?"

"Come on, let's go." She stood and gathered the debris from their picnic, putting everything in the backpack.

How could he say no to her? He found her intensity extremely attractive.

"All right, all right, give me that backpack," Josh said, grabbing it from her hands.

"Lead the way, Sheriff."

They climbed down the rocks and back to the sandy beach, dropping the bag into the kayak. Then they walked hand in hand, exchanging an occasional smile, until they reached the embankment to the woods above.

"You go up first," Josh said. "I'll help push you up—that way I can catch you if you slip."

Madi carefully managed the sloping edge, testing the dirt

and rocks with each step up the embankment. It was only about ten feet, so she made it up rather easily—mainly due to Josh's sheer strength in propelling her to the top. Josh swiftly climbed up in a few large steps and straightened up to meet her.

"I hope we see the deer again," Madi said.

The island was covered in spruce and fir balsam, along with ferns and wildflowers. It was very dense, and they stepped through a tangled web of undergrowth, weaving in and out of the trees.

"Do you know who owns this island?" Madi asked.

"Not specifically. Some of the local kayak guides pass by here on their water tours, which means it's most likely owned by one of the federal agencies or a conservation group. Many of these Maine islands are protected for nesting seabirds."

"That explains all the birds when we arrived."

"Exactly. There are a few hundred designated seabird-nesting islands, but thousands more with birds."

"What kinds of birds?" Madi asked.

"Terns, gulls, and cormorants, to name a few. A couple islands have puffins, but not this one."

"Can we go see the puffins this week?" Madi asked. "They're so cute."

"Sure. I have a friend who does tours out on Eastern Egg Rock. I'll call him."

They walked deeper into the overgrown island and felt the coolness of the air inside the dense trees. Josh was the first to spot the structure through the trees.

"Look, there's a building over there."

As they approached, Madi whispered, "It looks deserted."

"This island may have been privately owned at one time,"

Josh said.

The windows were boarded up, and the building looked run-down. At first glance, it appeared abandoned. However, when they got within a few feet, they looked at each other in bewilderment.

"Are you seeing what I'm seeing?" Madi asked.

"Yeah. It looks a lot like your boathouse."

With the exception of the French doors and back porch, this building was identical to the boathouse at the cottage. The windows were covered, so they couldn't look in. They walked around the whole perimeter, and noticed the outhouse built off to the side. Unlike the main section, the latrine was unlocked. Inside was a toilet with a deep underground hole. Next to the toilet was a sink. There was no running water or electricity, but on the floor stood a bucket and a few gallons of fresh water. When they saw the small hairbrush and soap on the sink, they realized someone had been there recently.

"We must be on private property. We should go," Josh said.

As they worked their way back to the kayak, Josh told Madi about how some of the islands in the area were privately owned by families who had been in Maine for generations. One of his favorites was Savoy Island in Linekin Bay, owned by the son of Bonnie June, the sweetest lady in Midcoast Maine. The family had turned the island into a day-trip excursion from Boothbay. Each summer season, tourists embarked on the family's large pontoon boat and headed to the island, where the owners and a group of teenage workers welcomed them for an old-fashioned clambake. While they prepared a generous meal of lobster, steamers, chowder, potatoes, and corn on the cob, the guests played badminton, horseshoes, and volleyball. This description brought back Madi's own dream of living on an island.

On the ride back, both of them were tired. *A good tired,* Madi thought. She was thinking about how sweet it was for Josh to plan this trip for her. He was such a nice, normal guy, not self-centered like so many of the city guys she knew—not because of where they were from, but because they were all fighting so hard to stand out in a sea of sameness. Josh seemed to love his job. Something he said had stayed with her: *You can live to work or you can work to live.* He had chosen the latter; had she?

"I can't believe that house is on the island; I never saw it when I was a kid. Then again, we never went that deep into the woods. We always fished from the rocks," Josh said.

"I wonder if it was built by the Walkers, since it's identical to the cottage boathouse," Madi said.

"Maybe it was Mr. Walker's fish house," Josh replied, "although I don't remember ever hearing about one."

"What if he owned the whole island back then?" Madi continued. "The other day I stopped at the library and looked at the town records."

"You did?"

"I can't believe Owls Head has a record of every resident since the 1800s in those books."

"The charm of a small town," Josh said wryly. "They know everything about you."

"Did you know that the Walkers left Owls Head with no forwarding address?" Madi asked.

"No, I didn't."

"You would think that as much as you guys know about

each other, someone would know where they went."

"You'd think."

"We should go back to the library and see if there's any record about who built that place on the island."

"Why?"

"Just for fun. I love finding out the history of the places I visit."

"You know, the other day when I was getting the grill, I saw some boxes in the barn. I think one or two of them said something about the previous owner. Maybe you can find a clue up there, Professor Plum," he teased.

She gave him a good splash with the paddle, and they fell silent for a while. Madi was daydreaming about the Walkers going to the island on weekends and making love in their secluded boathouse.

Josh was wondering why there hadn't been a forwarding address for the Walkers. He would ask his father about it.

As they approached the rocks on Madi's beach, they saw the golden retriever Madi had met the other day. He was running up and down the rocks, barking at them.

"That dog is so friendly—kind of like everyone else around here," Madi commented.

"I've never seen that dog before," Josh said, remembering that the neighbors had heard a dog barking on the morning of Kay's murder.

"Really? He's been hanging around my beach since I got here. Kind of like you," she teased.

Josh splashed her and she screamed.

"Seriously—how do people swim in this?" she asked.

CHAPTER TWELVE

He was waiting for her this time. Her car was in the drive, so she had to be somewhere close. She'd be back soon.

He heard his dog bark and headed for the crest. He crouched in the wildflowers behind the picnic table so he could see her approach. When the kayak came around the peninsula, he saw she wasn't alone. His blood began to boil as he realized they were the couple he'd seen on the island. He hadn't recognized her as she was facing away from him when he saw them having sex. He knew at this moment that she was just like his mother and sister. This was the last time he would allow a whore into his cottage.

He watched them from behind the boathouse. They pulled up the kayak and returned the gear to the porch. As they walked up to the cottage, the man with her pulled out a radio and spoke into it. Then he turned to her and they went into the cottage together.

When they emerged a few minutes later, he was dressed in different clothes and they each carried a set of keys.

After a quick kiss, she pulled her car into the spare parking spot to the side of the drive and he disappeared into the barn. She opened the barn door for him, and as his car backed out he could see it was a police vehicle.

The whore is banging the sheriff.

He would have to be very cautious with this one. When his sister had fallen to her death, it had been ruled an accident. But this one would involve the sheriff. He would need to make sure he covered his tracks well—even better than the others.

* * *

After Madi had showered, she couldn't resist the urge to check out the boxes in the barn. She had no idea how long Josh would be gone. He'd gotten a lead that Bill Andrews had been spotted in a bar on the New Hampshire coast, and he was going to investigate.

She looked around the old barn, and above her in the loft she saw what Josh had mentioned. Among the stack of boxes, one was labeled PREVIOUS OWNER. She ascended the unsteady, narrow staircase. Apparently the current owner hadn't touched this barn, as it certainly looked, smelled, and creaked like it was nearly seventy years old. She carefully tested each step before going further, fearing the stairs might cave under her weight.

She found a spot near the only window at the front of the barn and settled in. She pulled off the duct tape and opened the box to find that it was filled with folders of documents. Inside were old bills, receipts, and warranties for various appliances and household items. There was nothing of major consequence.

Madi came across a folder marked HOUSE CLOSING and

looked inside. The owner's name was Sarah Wilson, just as the librarian had said; no other name on the deed. Her previous address was in Connecticut. Ms. Wilson had acquired the property from the Penobscot Regional Bank.

There was nothing in the box about the original property, no blueprints or plans. Madi was hoping it had been left in the home and found by Ms. Wilson. There must have been an original deed, but maybe in the 1940s deeds were kept by the town rather than by the owner. She hadn't looked very closely at the property information in the library the other day; maybe it had said something about the island, and she hadn't noticed.

Near the bottom of the box, Madi at first overlooked a folder, since it said OLD HOUSE. She assumed it was from the lady's home in Connecticut. But when she pulled it out to see if there were any folders beneath, a thin, bound journal slid out.

She read the first passage, dated March 19, 2001:

I can't believe I'm finally here. Being in Maine brings back so many childhood memories. The cottage is in much disarray, but now that I'm retired I have plenty of time to work on it. I know it will take a while, since my retirement funds are limited. I will have to do a little at a time.

The boathouse is a disaster as well. It needs a total cleaning from top to bottom. After the closing, the real estate agent told me that a homeless person had been staying in it, which explains the odor. Part of me feels horrible that they chased him out when I bought the place.

I have thought recently about mother and father. My heart aches for them. I think they would be happy to see me here.

Carrying the journal with her, Madi closed up the box and climbed down the stairs. She changed into a bathing suit and cover-up. Her plan was to get a tan on the boathouse porch and read some more about Sarah Wilson's retirement.

The weather was amazing again. *If Maine had weather like this all summer,* she thought, *this place would be much more crowded.* It occurred to her that she had hardly seen any people on the beach this week. The adorable gray house to the left of the boathouse looked empty. The rental agent had told her the owners were seasonal, and only came for weekends. They hadn't been there last weekend, but Friday was the Fourth of July, so perhaps they would arrive soon.

She opened the journal and settled into her Adirondack chair. Many of the entries described the condition of the cottage, and how Sarah had spent much of the first few months cleaning and painting. She wrote that the larger jobs like the roof and plumbing would have to wait; she couldn't afford to replace those big-ticket items. From what Madi could discern, the second floor did not yet have a bathroom; that must have been an addition by the current owner.

An entry on October 12, 2004, was the first time Sarah mentioned anyone in her family besides her parents:

I received a letter from my brother. I never thought I would hear from him again. He claims he has recovered and wants to come visit me.

Recovered? Had he been an alcoholic, perhaps, or a drug addict?

Madi read on. After a dozen or more entries about the house and other extraneous details of her days, Sarah mentions her brother again.

Today I opened the door to see my brother standing there. Although the years have aged him, I still recognized him immediately. Terrified, I asked him what he was doing here, and how he'd found me. He said he knew I had come back to Maine, but didn't explain how. He said things had changed and he wasn't the same person he was back then. He had been through counseling and was being treated with medication.

I was fearful of trusting him. I told him I didn't know if I could forgive him, and he said he understood. He asked if perhaps he could visit occasionally, as he lived nearby. I told him I didn't know, but the thought of him being close by is unsettling. How close, I wonder? And, what would Mother and Father think about him being here after what he did?

Madi didn't know what to think about this entry. What had Sarah's brother done? Maybe he'd stolen from them . . . but then why would she be terrified to see him? She kept reading, wanting to learn more about Sarah's life.

* * *

The man emerged out of the water and placed his gear in the woods. She was reading on the porch again, and he was sure the sheriff was gone. At the top of the crest he made himself visible and waved to her on the porch.

"Hello," she called. Madi recognized him as the man in the wet suit that she'd met the other day.

"Great day for a swim!" he hollered.

"Yeah, if you have a wet suit." She laughed. "The water is a little frigid in this part of the country."

"Have you seen all the sea glass that washed ashore last night?" he asked her.

"No, I didn't notice that when I was down there before," she responded.

"Come on down—I'll show you how to find the best pieces."

Madi took a break from reading and started down to the

beach. When she reached the sand, he was already bent over at the shore.

"Ohh, it's freezing," Madi said as she tried to walk out to where he stood, knee-deep, his arms under the water. Laughing, he told her to give it a minute—she would adjust.

"You have to fish around under the sand, like this," he said, pulling out a piece of sea glass that he'd hidden under the ankle of his suit.

"Oh my gosh, that's beautiful," she said of the cobalt-blue wedge of softened glass. He handed it to her. "It's so smooth," she said.

"It's yours to keep," he offered.

"Thank you. I just can't get over how nice everyone is around here—not at all like Manhattan."

"How so?"

"Well, everyone really keeps to themselves there. They're not nearly as welcoming," she explained.

Madi bent over further and spread her hands under the sand, feeling for pieces of smooth glass. He waited until she was totally engrossed in her task before he positioned himself behind her.

"I can't find anything," she said, looking up at him. His goggles were off now, and she looked at his eyes closely for the first time. A chill came over her. *Where had she seen those eyes before?*

"It's mine," he said as he stepped toward her.

"Did you find a piece?" she asked, looking down at his clenched hands.

Suddenly, they heard a child's voice carrying over the water. "Grandma, come in with me!"

They looked up to see a little girl running toward the water, and behind her, a family arranging chairs and towels on the beach.

"It's too cold for Grandma, sweetie," an older woman yelled back.

"Pleeeease," the little girl pleaded. "Look, those people are in the water."

Madi smiled and waved at them, realizing they had come from the gray house. The family from Massachusetts had arrived for the holiday weekend, just as the rental agent predicted.

"Hi there," Madi said to the girl. "We were just looking for sea glass. The water is freezing, though."

The man told Madi he had to go, quickly said good-bye, and headed up the path toward the boathouse. She heard a dog bark as he disappeared into the woods.

She looked down at the glass and rubbed it between her fingers, picturing his eyes in her head. He had reminded her of someone. *Who was it?*

* * *

The young bartender at the Old Salt in Hampton Beach insisted that he meet with Josh away from the restaurant.

"It's a small town," he explained.

Once they were settled in a local coffee shop, Josh began his questioning. "I understand you may have served Bill Andrews yesterday afternoon."

"Yes, sir."

"But you're not certain?"

"He was wearing a baseball hat and sunglasses."

"What made you think it was him?"

"Well, after he had a few beers at the bar, he began talking a bit. He pulled out a huge wad of cash to pay his tab, and when he noticed me looking at it, he bragged that he had inherited it from a relative that had croaked."

"What else did he say?"

"He went on a bit about how his ex-wife—'ex-bitch,' as he called her—wanted a piece of it. When I asked him what he was going to do about it, he said it was already taken care of. I asked if he'd paid her off, and he said, 'No, I got rid of her.' "

The bartender continued. "Of course, I laughed it off at the time; he wasn't the first drunk guy to mouth off a bunch of bullshit at my bar. But then I remembered the story on the news of the woman in Owls Head who was killed by her ex-husband. I went online this morning and looked at the picture of him, and I think it's the same guy."

Josh went back to the bar and interviewed the rest of the staff who'd been working the day before. A couple of servers said they had never seen Andrews there before. He left his card with the manager and the bartender, and then went to the local sheriff's department. Afterwards, he headed to the closest marina to see if Andrews had tried to get out on the water with any of the local lobstermen. It would be harder to find him if he was out on a boat.

Josh didn't bother stopping at any of the hotels; surely Andrews would have used a fake name anywhere he stayed. With the sheer number of tourists this time of year, it would be like finding a needle in a haystack.

Josh left his card with folks around the marina and started back home about six o'clock. He had a three-hour drive ahead of him if he abided by the speed limit. By now, though, he was really missing Madi; he considered whether he might have to turn the lights on a few times.

CHAPTER THIRTEEN

She had seen his eyes—he knew that for sure. He recognized her subconscious look of fear. In fact, he could smell it. It was the same vile odor that had erupted from his sister when she'd seen him at the top of the stairs. She had begged for her life, just as his mother had. *Thomas*, they had each cried—*Please*. Selfish as always. Always concerned about themselves. They'd never given a damn about him. Did they care if he ever found out who his real father was? Did anyone on this godforsaken Earth care that his mother had played the part of the dedicated wife but was actually the town slut?

He closed his eyes and tried to maintain control. He had to remain calm so he could get rid of the whore in his house. He retrieved his kayak from the woods and headed back to the island.

* * *

Madi introduced herself to her neighbors on the beach.

The owner was Anna, aka Grandma. She and her husband Dave lived in Wellesley, and they had just arrived for the holiday weekend. Anna's daughter Gwen, son-in-law Peter, and granddaughter Gabby had come in from Jersey. It was an annual tradition.

Madi sat with Anna and Gwen for a bit, exchanging stories about their backgrounds and laughing at little Gabby, who was loving the water and searching for shells. She didn't seem to notice the frigid temperature one bit. The men had gone to town for some groceries so they could have a cookout that evening. They invited Madi to join them. Having no idea when Josh would be back, she gladly accepted.

Madi had a lot of friends in Manhattan, and loved nothing more than enjoying good food and company. This town was certainly lacking in the entertainment area, and Madi was ready for a social gathering. It had been nearly a week since she had been around a group of people.

She showered and dressed, throwing on a bright yellow sundress and twisting her hair up. When she was just about ready, her cell phone rang. It was Josh.

"Well, hello, Sheriff."

"Well, hello, yourself," Josh said.

"Are you back?"

"I've just crossed into Maine. I'll be home in a couple of hours."

"Perfect," she replied. "I'm going to the neighbors' for dinner right now, so maybe I can see you after."

"The neighbors?"

"Across the street. They just got here from Massachusetts. Very nice family. Do you know them?" Madi asked. Her voice was teasing, a reminder of her earlier jest that he didn't know whose dog she had met on her beach.

"Yes, I know Anna and Dave Landon, smarty-pants," Josh said, laughing, then asked, "So I can come over later?"

"Is this a booty call?"

"No, I just wanna cuddle," he quickly shot back.

"I'm not that kind of girl," she said archly before hanging up.

With the last bottle of white wine from the fridge in tow, Madi walked across the lane.

* * *

When Josh arrived later that night, he found Madi on the neighbors' porch. He had gone home to change out of his uniform, and it was nearly ten o'clock.

As he approached, he said, "Folks, it's getting late. I don't want to have to call the cops on you for disturbing the peace."

Dave Landon stood up and shook Josh's hand with a laugh. "How are you, Josh?"

"I'm great, Dave. Nice to see you."

He kissed Anna on the cheek and said hello to Gwen, Peter, and Gabby. He remarked that he hadn't seen them up in a while.

Dave replied, "I've been traveling a lot for work. I hear we missed some tragic events here in Owls Head."

Josh nodded.

"That's so sad about Kay," Anna said. "It's hard to believe that the suspect made bail."

Madi broke into the conversation, asking, "Did you find Andrews, Josh?"

"I'm afraid not, but we believe he's down in New

Hampshire. Hopefully he'll stay put long enough for someone to identify him again."

Dave offered Josh a beer and they all chatted for a bit. Madi seemed to have made a connection with Anna and Gwen, because they were talking like old friends. While Josh conversed with Dave and Peter, he occasionally exchanged glances with Madi. He loved her outgoing personality. She was extremely comfortable talking with people, and they with her. She had a way of communicating that was both direct and warm at the same time.

It was eleven o'clock when the conversation started to die down. Gwen had gone to tuck Gabby in a while ago, and he saw Madi squelch a yawn once or twice. Josh wondered about Anna and Dave, and what Madi had told the couple about the two of them. Should he pretend to head out and then sneak back to the cottage? Just when he was struggling with how to handle things, Madi saved the day.

"Josh, you must be exhausted," she said. "You probably need to go home and get some shut-eye."

"I am pretty beat," he said, playing along.

"I'm tired too," Anna admitted.

"Thanks so much for inviting me to dinner; I enjoyed it so much," Madi said as she stood up.

"You're welcome, dear," Anna said, giving Madi a hug.

After more than a few good-byes and plans to get together again, the two of them headed up the drive to the lane.

"My place?" Josh asked.

"Absolutely," Madi answered quickly.

She locked up the cottage and met Josh in the barn after going out the back laundry-room door.

"Are we in high school?" she asked Josh when she slid

down in the passenger seat so she wouldn't be seen in his car.

"We're in a town with a population of fifteen hundred. Same thing."

Fifteen hundred? The size of my high school graduating class, Madi thought.

* * *

Madi hadn't been to Josh's house since their first night together—Monday, only two days before. How could that be? It felt like she had known him forever. It couldn't have been only two nights ago that they had first made love. She ran it over in her mind while Josh was driving.

"Cat got your tongue?" he asked, yanking Madi from her thoughts.

"No, just tired. The days here last forever."

"Not long enough, if you ask me," Josh said, grabbing her hand in his while he steered with his left hand. She looked down at his hand holding hers and gave him a smile.

They were so exhausted that they didn't make love that night. What they did was even better, Madi thought. They cuddled like Josh had joked about earlier. Madi grew drowsy as Josh told her a bedtime story—the legend of Spot, the lighthouse dog. He was a springer spaniel belonging to Augustus B. Hamor, lighthouse keeper in the 1930s. Spot would pull the rope that rang the fog bell with his teeth, to warn approaching vessels.

One stormy night, the mailboat almost ran aground at Owls Head. With so much snow on the ground, Spot couldn't find the rope to pull the fog bell, so he barked constantly to warn the captain in time to steer clear of the rocks. The dog was said to be buried on the side of the hill near the former location of the fog bell. A gravestone next to the house bore his name.

Madi fell asleep in Josh's arms, feeling happy and at home. In a moment, she was dreaming again of being on the beach, skipping rocks again. This time the voice she heard was a familiar one. *Like this,* he said, taking her arm in his and flinging the rock out over the water. Her dream went on for a bit, with Josh behind her, cheering her on, telling her she could do it. It reminded her of her father, who'd told her that she could do anything she wanted. This time, though, she knew Josh didn't mean she wasn't worthy. She knew he thought she was amazing.

She turned to him in her dream, but the man standing before her wasn't Josh; it was the man in the wet suit. She couldn't see his face behind the hood of the suit and the snorkel, but she could see his eyes, dark and penetrating.

She woke up in a sweat with clear knowledge of where she'd seen those eyes before: They were the eyes she'd seen in the window of the cottage.

"Josh—Josh!" she called, feeling for him on the bed. *Not again,* she thought, running out to the kitchen.

Another note sat on the table.

"No!" she exclaimed as she flipped it open. The note read: *They have Bill Andrews in custody. Had to go to New Hampshire. Love, Josh.*

New Hampshire? Madi was confused and shaken. It was just yesterday afternoon that the man in the wet suit had been showing her the sea glass. She was certain they were the same eyes she'd seen in the window when Josh was outside, running after Andrews. How could he be in New Hampshire when she'd just seen him yesterday at the beach? And the night at the window, when was it that she'd seen him standing there—before or after she had heard Josh run by?

She grabbed her cell to call Josh. It was five a.m.

* * *

"Hi there, sleepyhead," Josh said as he answered his phone, surprised. "What are you doing up so early?"

"Josh, I need to talk to you."

She sounded serious, and Josh's tone changed immediately to one of concern. "What's the matter?"

"I had this dream. We were on the beach, but it wasn't you, it was him. I mean, I saw him, Josh." Madi spoke so fast and frantically that Josh had no idea what she was trying to say.

"Slow down, Madi—what are you talking about?"

"It was Andrews. He's the man in the wet suit. I saw him yesterday!"

"How? Where?"

"On the beach, yesterday afternoon."

"Madi, honey, it can't be Andrews. The sheriff's department in Hampton Beach has had surveillance on him since yesterday. They picked him up this morning at a lobster dock."

Josh wasn't listening to her. "His eyes, Josh—the man in the wet suit and the man in the window have the same eyes. He was the man I saw in the window the other night at the cottage, when you were outside looking for him. He's the same man I've told you about. I swear, they are one and the same."

"No, Madi—Andrews just has a similar physical appearance as the man you told me about. Perhaps they look somewhat alike. Your mind is probably playing tricks on you. All this murder stuff can do that to a person."

Her fear was turning to frustration. He wasn't taking her seriously, and she suddenly felt stupid. She fell silent.

"Madi, listen to me. Turn on the news. They should have a picture of Andrews on there by now, from the arrest. You can see what he looks like—that it's not the same person. It can't be."

She wasn't listening. Instead, she was putting the wall back up—the one she'd let down sometime earlier that week. It was her modus operandi. In the past, whenever she had started to trust a man's feelings for her, something would happen to make her retreat. Josh had made Madi feel as though he didn't believe in her, and that was the one thing Madi needed most of all.

Maybe it was time to release, she thought sadly.

CHAPTER FOURTEEN

Madi showered and collected her things. She left Josh's note on the table and grabbed the bike she had seen in his second bedroom. As she rode away from the house and pedaled the four miles back to her cottage, she decided to put the whole incident behind her.

By the time she stopped at the general store, she had made up her mind that this thing with Josh had gone too far, and it was time to start thinking of Saturday. The fact she was so upset that he'd brushed her off was proof that her feelings for him had grown beyond those of a harmless summer fling. *Had she lost her mind?* The last thing she needed right now was a long-distance relationship. In fact, she didn't need *any* relationship; she needed to spend the rest of her vacation clearing her head and getting ready to return to the pressures of the advertising world. If that meant she needed to put the brakes on this thing with Josh, then that's what she would do.

A cup of coffee and one of Lynne's pumpkin whoopie pies was just the thing to change Madi's mood. Today she would start anew, enjoying the solitude of the cottage and the peacefulness of the boathouse porch. It would be better this way, she decided, especially for Josh. His feelings for her were obviously strong, and she didn't want to hurt him come Saturday.

From the general store she could see the librarian unlocking the front door and heading in. It was almost nine a.m. She walked over, leaned the bike against the library wall, and opened the door.

"Good morning," Madi said.

"Hello, dear—nice to see you again."

"Are you open?" she asked.

"Officially, not until nine-thirty, but you're welcome to come in."

"Thanks," she said, and headed straight for the shelves that housed the history of Owls Head residents. She pulled the 1940s volume off the shelf and went back to the Walkers' page. There was nothing about Monroe Island anywhere.

She set her sights on the old periodicals. The simplicity of the newspaper from that era made her laugh. The ads were humorous, and reminded Madi of the ones she had seen on the Internet, positioning women as housewives whose only job was to serve their husbands after a long trip out to sea.

Not much was happening around Owls Head at that time. The news consisted of local events, town meetings, and seafaring information. She smiled when she read the weekly articles written by Douglas Larabee, the lighthouse keeper. Her thoughts turned to Josh, and she realized her anger was starting to subside. *Still,* she thought, *it's time to detach.*

On September 30, 1962, an obituary headline caught her eye: MARGARET AND THOMAS WALKER SR. OF OWLS HEAD

DIED ON MONDAY.

What—they died? They didn't move away? Were they in an accident? How come no one around here seems to know that? And what about the kids—what happened to them? She looked back again at the original volume and calculated the kids' ages at the time of their parents' deaths. They were nineteen and fifteen.

She scoured the rest of the papers surrounding that date and found nothing more about the Walkers or their children.

* * *

The sky had gotten a little hazy. Madi knew of the infamous fog roll-ins, but had been blessed with mostly clear skies this whole week. Josh had told her that when there was fog offshore during the morning, it could either burn off by noon, or a sou'wester could sweep in during the afternoon and blanket you in no time. Since the sun was obscured overhead, she decided this would be a great day to do the touristy thing in town.

She parked Josh's bike in the barn and retrieved her keys from the cottage. In the car, she began thinking of home, and of Kristen. She dialed her cell and her trusted friend answered on the first ring.

"What do ya know? If it isn't my long-lost best friend!" Kristen exclaimed.

"Hey, Kris!"

"Hi, Madi, how's the vay-cay?"

"It's been great. The house I am renting is adorable. All white furniture with pillows that have shells on them." She chuckled. "Totally the opposite of New York loft."

"Sounds sweet. So what have you been doing?"

Madi told her about kayaking to the island, biking to the general store, and the charming town of Rockland. Then, she nonchalantly threw in one more small detail and quietly waited for the eruption on the other end.

"What do you mean, you *met* someone?" Kristen shrilled with obvious excitement.

"Just a guy who lives around here." Madi played coy with Kristen, knowing full well that her best friend would want every torrid detail. Something happened when friends got engaged; suddenly they felt the need to try and hook you up with every single guy they knew.

"You're not getting off that easy, Madi. Where did you meet him? Not at a bar, I hope."

"Please, woman, there's no nightlife here. Like, at all. Actually, he's the sheriff of Owls Head."

"The sheriff! Are you kidding me? What did you do, get arrested for kayaking too fast?" Kristen was going to have her fun with this.

"Not exactly. A woman was murdered the first night I was here, and he came to the door to ask me some questions."

"You're not serious."

"I am."

"Oh my God, Madi—a murder? Are you safe there?" Her friend had turned from amused to concerned in an instant.

"Don't worry, Kristen. The woman's ex-husband is the suspect, and Josh is actually down in New Hampshire today, arresting the guy. So, I'm fine."

"Josh, huh? How many times have you seen this Josh? Have you guys . . . ya know . . . ?"

Madi laughed. "You are too funny. Yes, we have, if you must know."

"This sounds serious."

"No, it's not. Just a catch-and-release." They both laughed again. "But he *is* quite a hottie."

"Pray tell," Kristen begged, and Madi described Josh to her friend. She was careful not to sound too smitten in her depiction of his beautiful blue eyes, his strapping body, or his gentle, sweet lips. Those kinds of adjectives she would keep to herself.

Thankfully it wasn't long before they moved on to Kristen and her developing wedding plans. Just as Kris started complaining about her future mother-in-law not minding her own business, Madi pulled into the museum parking lot.

She casually interrupted Kristen's drawn-out rant. "Hey, Kris, I'm heading in to look at some artwork. Can I call you Saturday when I'm on my way home?"

"Yeah, sure. Make sure to say hi to the sheriff for me."

* * *

Stepping inside the Farnsworth Museum, Madi was immediately impressed with the beauty of the lobby. Having visited every major museum in New York City, she had become somewhat of a museum aficionado. She was surprised to see the world-class collections listed on the rack brochure at the front desk.

"Good morning," the curator greeted her softly. "Will you please sign our guestbook?"

Madi penned her name and handed the entrance fee to the lady.

"Thank you, Miss Lyons," the woman said, gleaning her name from the guestbook. She proceeded to tell Madi about the collections, describing the six galleries in the Farnsworth and the two located in the Wyeth Center. Madi had not realized the museum was sprawled over a two-block radius. She was in her element.

The woman at the desk was looking at her a bit oddly; turning her head to the side, she asked, "Are you the young lady staying at the Walker cottage in Owls Head?"

My goodness, do I have a sign on my forehead or what?

"Umm, yes," she answered in a perplexed tone.

"Oh." The woman's voice piped up an octave as she announced, "I'm Judy Daniels, Joshua's mother."

Madi didn't know what to say. News *had* traveled fast. Certainly Josh hadn't told her of their relationship. He had very specifically confessed that he usually didn't tell his mom when he met someone because she would try to marry him off after the first date. Madi was positive that Lynne, the general store owner, must have told Mrs. Daniels about her.

"Nice to meet you," Madi said, offering her hand.

"Let me know if there is anything I can help you with, anything at all."

Madi thanked her before heading off to the first gallery.

The Farnsworth was a fabulous celebration of American artwork. Roaming from room to room, Madi was transported through time, viewing American impressionism, realism, modernism, and folk art. Important artists' works from Rockwell Kent, Winslow Homer, Edward Hopper, and Robert Henri adorned the walls.

Most intriguing to Madi was the Wyeth Center, featuring the artwork of three generations of Maine natives, N. C., Andrew, and Jamie Wyeth. One of her favorites, Andrew Wyeth's *Christina's World*, had captivated Madi since her days in art history class. The woman stretched out on the lawn in front of her house had always made Madi wonder if she was lying there because she was hurt; was she crippled? She learned here that Christina Olson and her husband were good friends of Wyeth's, and their home was a common subject of his paintings. The home itself was now part of the Farnsworth Museum, open for tours in the town of Cushing, a bit down coast. *Tomorrow's adventure, perhaps,* she thought.

Madi spent nearly an hour gazing at the extensive collection of Andrew Wyeth's temperas, watercolors, dry-brush paintings, and drawings in the main museum building. She decided the temperas were her favorite, with their attention to detail and incredible realism. Every stroke of grass, every grain of wood, every shadow was apparent in the nearly photographic paintings.

Across the street, she toured pieces from Andrew's father, N. C., and son, Jamie. The latter reminded her of an older version of Josh. Something about the Maine coast seemed to give men a distinctly rugged look. Jamie was more experimental than his father and grandfather, painting with oils, gouaches, and combined mediums. She liked his Maine depictions and his political portraitures. He had painted a great deal on Monhegan Island, and now lived in the solitude of Southern Island after years of pursuing art in New York City and D.C. His bio reminded her of Robert Rauschenberg, another of her favorites, a contemporary artist who had run with Andy Warhol and Jasper Johns back in the day, but settled on tropical Captiva Island, Florida, for his later years. Jamie knew Warhol, and Madi wondered whether he and Robert had known each other.

After she exited the nineteenth-century church that housed

N. C. and Jamie's work, she toured the Farnsworth Homestead, a Greek-revival home with Victorian interiors that had belonged to the family whose name now graced the museum.

Madi was peeking into one of the two servants' rooms when her cell phone broke the silence of the historic structure. It was Josh. She quickly hit the quiet button, remembering the NO CELL PHONES sign at the front door of the house. When she emerged from the dark home into the bright sunlight of midday, she listened to her voicemail: "Hi, Madi, it's me, Josh. I'm sorry if I upset you this morning; I didn't mean to be insensitive." Josh paused, then added, "I hope I can see you tonight. We only have two days left. Don't be mad. Call me."

She smiled at his sincerity. She realized he was just being logical. All this murder stuff was messing with her mind. She decided to wait a bit longer before calling him back. She needed to think about how she was going to handle things between now and Saturday.

* * *

Madi was starving. She had enjoyed the museum longer than anticipated and it was nearly two o'clock already. When she reached Main Street, she turned north to see what she could find for lunch. There was the coffee shop behind her, and a diner across the street. On the corner straight ahead was the Black Bull Tavern. The sign with the handwritten specials boasted a burger on focaccia bread; that, and a cold beer, sounded perfect, Madi decided.

She entered the second door to the bar and sat on a stool

near the front of the restaurant. With the large storefront window, Madi had a front-row seat designed for people watching, one of her favorite pastimes in Manhattan. After a few minutes and nearly no passersby, Madi realized the number of people hanging out in this Maine town was underwhelming. She turned to the television, which was showing a Red Sox game. *Probably not a good idea to ask to change the station to the Yankees game in this neck of the woods.*

A sign caught her eye near the cash register. WANTED: BILL ANDREWS, FOR THE MURDER OF TWO BLACK BULL EMPLOYEES. Below that was a picture of Andrews. One glance and she knew Josh was right: Andrews wasn't the man in the wet suit. While both were silver-haired and tall, Andrews was far more weatherworn than the wet-suit man. *Her imagination was clearly playing tricks on her, like Josh had said.*

"Excuse me—Madi, is it?" a voice asked from behind.

Who knew her here? She turned to see that Josh's mother had entered the bar. *Oh my God.*

"I thought I saw you in the window," she said, smiling.

"Well, hello again, Mrs. Daniels."

"Call me Judy, please."

"Okay, Judy," Madi said awkwardly.

"I was just on my lunch hour," she explained. "Did you enjoy the museum?"

"It was fabulous," Madi said. "I love Andrew Wyeth's work. I studied him in college."

"Did you now? He's an important part of Maine history. Have you been to the Olson House?"

"Not yet, but I was thinking of going tomorrow." After a moment, she realized she was being rude. "Would you like to sit down?" she asked, pulling out the stool next to her.

"Actually, I was going to get a bite—as long as you don't mind?" Judy asked.

"Not at all." Madi gave her best performance. *This is dangerous.*

Madi and Judy chatted while their lunch was being prepared. Madi was mindful not to mention too much time spent with Josh as they discussed her stay in Maine thus far. Judy was a wealth of information about the area's history and its long heritage of art. She was a naturally attractive woman, Madi noticed, wearing a short-sleeved pink sweater and white pants, and very little makeup.

Madi was enjoying her stories until Judy suddenly steered the conversation to her son. She knew the topic was inevitable, but how far would the woman pry? She almost laughed as she imagined telling Judy about her catch-and-release philosophy.

"Madi, can I tell you something?" Judy leaned over and lowered her voice so Madi could hardly hear her.

"Umm, sure." *What's she about to say?*

"Josh is quite taken with you," she whispered. "He told me."

"He told you that?" She worried she was being baited. She knew how parents could be. *Had he really told his mother about her?*

"The truth is, my son never tells me about anyone he is dating. You must be very special."

Dating? Is that what we're doing?

"Joshua doesn't open up to many women. And he's not one to have a casual fling."

Oh Lord, where is this going?

Judy continued after a moment of thought. "He wouldn't tell me about you if you weren't important to him. He'd be too afraid I would interfere in the relationship."

Now why on earth would he think that?

"Mrs. Daniels, with all due respect, we just met."

"I know, Madi, but I just thought you should know how he feels about you before you leave."

"I meant, you and I just met, so this is a little awkward for me," Madi went on. "What do you mean, how he feels about me?"

"He can't stop talking about you, dear. Believe me, a mother knows when her son is falling in love."

For the remainder of the meal, Madi wondered if the huge smile she could feel pasted on her face was as evident to Judy as it was to her. Despite herself, the thought of Josh being in love with her made her happy. Surprisingly happy.

Madi insisted on picking up the tab for their lunch, and Judy thanked her effusively before heading back to the museum.

Now what am I going to do? Madi thought as she left the restaurant. She was afraid of getting hurt. And yet, she was also afraid of losing Josh.

CHAPTER FIFTEEN

Madi had yet to call him back, and it was after three. *She must be pretty mad,* Josh thought. He would make it up to her and take her out for a nice dinner. As soon as he finished this huge pile of paperwork on the Andrews case, he would try her again. Hopefully he would hear from her by then.

Josh picked up the phone and called Bellissimo in Rockland and made a reservation for eight p.m. It was one of his favorite restaurants, owned by his good friend, a graduate of the Culinary Institute in New York. She and her husband had turned their hundred-year-old Victorian farmhouse into an elegant restaurant, with its own two-acre garden and hand-raised livestock. Josh had long been a fan of his friend's inspired cooking, and he hoped Madi would be impressed with her regional cuisine. He also called Lynne and asked if she had any fresh flowers. When she said she did, he told her he'd pick them up before she closed at seven.

Josh's thoughts inevitably returned to the case.

Bill Andrews was a real piece of work, hardwired to be a

rugged lobsterman, as rough as they come, and with a serious drinking problem. Men like that were not at all uncommon in these parts. Years of being out on the cold coastal waters doing grueling work produced some less than savory personalities. Andrews had an anger problem to boot, and his ex-wife had left him because he'd started to push her around. During the investigation, some of her family and friends had reported that his drinking had gotten worse over the past few years.

Madi had been understandably shaken up the night the trespasser was outside of the cottage—presumably Andrews—insisting she'd seen him through the window. And today she'd woken up from a bad dream, thinking the man she'd seen through the window was the man in the wet suit she'd met by the boathouse. Josh was sure the anxiety over Kay's murder and seeing the flashlight outside had led to her nightmare. Dreams were always a jumble of reality and fantasy. He had tried to reassure her, but she'd been quite adamant that they were one and the same man.

Now that Andrews was in jail, he hoped Madi would be able to relax a little. He wanted her last two days here to be happy ones. He was going to do his best to make sure of it.

* * *

After having lunch with Josh's sweet mom, Madi forgave him for not believing her that morning. Plus, she knew from seeing Bill Andrews's photo in the tavern that the man in the wet suit was not Andrews. It was silly of her to have gotten so angry. She knew it was just her defenses kicking in; she had been denying the depth of her feelings for Josh.

Josh couldn't stop talking about her, his mother had told

Madi. Judy had also said Josh couldn't imagine what he would do when Madi left. *Was this really happening?*

This whole week had been surreal. First, a murder; then, she meets and has an affair with the sheriff. As wonderful as it had been, being with Josh, how unfair was it, to meet a great guy who lives four hundred miles away. What would happen after Saturday? If she didn't cut it off, would they exchange daily phone calls and texts, and plan occasional visits? How long before the novelty wore off? It wasn't the first time she had tried a long-distance relationship. They didn't work. She needed to figure out what to do.

She returned to Mahalas Lane at about 4:30 p.m. and pulled the car up to the cottage door. She planned to unpack her souvenirs from the museum store and then head down to the boathouse with her new sketchpad and colored pencils. Josh would be finished working soon, so she figured she'd give him a call once she got settled on the porch. Before she made the call, though, she wanted to pour herself a glass of wine and think about what Judy had said. She had said her son was "falling in love" with Madi. The last thing Madi wanted to do was make leaving on Saturday harder than it already was going to be, but the truth was, she really wanted to see him tonight.

As afraid as she was to admit it, she knew she was falling for Josh as well.

*   *   *

The hair on his arms and the back of his neck rose as he heard the tires roll over the gravel. Peeking out from the small laundry-room window, he saw she was back. And alone. He slipped into the master bedroom closet and wrapped the

121

bandana around his wrist. The front door creaked open and he heard the screen door slam. Keys were dropped onto a table, and the old floorboards creaked under her feet. He saw her figure pass the closet doors, and through the slats he watched her drop her bags onto the floor. When she bent over to rummage through the larger of the two bags, he carefully slid the door open and stepped out behind her.

Madi was reaching down to grab the pad and pencils out of the shopping bag when she heard a creak in the floorboard behind her. Jerking her body straight up, she felt a cold, hard object pressed against her lower back. Faster than she could respond, a hand covered her mouth as she let out a muffled cry. A man's voice growled in her ear, "Don't make a sound."

She felt the pressure of the object in her back as he pressed harder. *A gun.* Her body stiffened, and she stood as still as she could, her mind already racing with thoughts of trying to get away.

"We're going to take a walk outside. If you say a word, I will kill you." His voice was low and devoid of emotion. A chill ran through her veins. She had no doubt he meant what he said. She nodded in understanding and he turned her without removing his hand from her mouth. His face was very close to the back of her neck; the only thing separating them was the butt of his gun.

When they reached the laundry-room door, he said, "We're going to walk across the driveway and into the woods. Don't try anything stupid. Understand?" She nodded, and he removed his hand from her mouth. He reached his arm around her to open the door. Outside, he told her to stop while he shut the door behind him. He kept the gun pressed into her back and shoved her forward.

About ten steps onto the wooded property next to the driveway, he told her to walk to her left, to the edge of the lane. "We're going to cross the road and go down to the water. If anyone sees us, just act natural, like we're going for a stroll. Got it?"

Madi nodded. Her mind was a speedway of thoughts. *Should she scream—try to run? Where was he taking her? What did he want?*

They reached the rocky coast to the south of the cottage. There was no more beach here, and it was slippery wet rocks all the way down to the risen tide. As she stepped out onto the rocks, she felt him place a rolled bandana around her face and in her mouth. He had moved the gun from her back long enough to tie the bandana behind her head. She wanted to run, but she was standing on wet rocks. It would be impossible to get back onto solid ground fast enough. And if she tried to run, he could easily shoot her.

He pushed the gun into her back again and she moved forward, carefully stepping from rock to rock, trying to keep her balance while he followed behind her. Near the water, she could see a very long tandem kayak onshore. Her eyes widened in shock when she saw what stood beside it: the friendly golden retriever from the beach. *Oh my God,* she thought. *That dog . . . it's his.*

He told her not to move while he went to her right side. It was her first glance at him. The wet suit was the first thing she saw before he looked at her with those dark, empty eyes. *It was him.*

He instructed her to get in the boat and gently shoved it off of the rocks. He climbed in behind her and the dog, tied her hands behind her back with rope, and began to paddle. She could hear the dog panting, and this, combined with the

123

ominous sound of the waves hitting the front of the kayak, gave her a sinking feeling that she would not be coming back to shore.

* * *

Josh tried to reach Madi again, but she still wouldn't answer. He would go to the cottage with his flowers and beg her forgiveness. He had upset her, and hoped to make things right tonight at Bellissimo. The owners would make sure he had one of the best tables in the house, along with a beautiful meal. Madi was from the Big Apple, and Josh assumed she had dined at some of the finest restaurants. He wanted desperately to impress her.

Pulling in the driveway, he saw the rental car parked by the front door. He parked behind it, stepped around the car, and knocked on the front door. After a second and then a third knock, he called out her name. When he turned the knob, it was unlocked, so he let himself in.

"Madi?" he called as he walked through the living room toward the back bedroom. *Could she be napping at nearly six-thirty?*

In the bedroom, he saw her purse laying on the bed and two shopping bags on the floor. He recognized the one from the museum gift shop and hoped his mother hadn't been working today. He climbed the stairs and hollered her name. Perhaps she was taking a bath.

When he didn't find her in the cottage, he went to check the boathouse and the beach. It was getting too dark for a bike ride, so she was probably reading on the porch or walking on the beach. The sun was beginning to set behind the cottage, and the sky over the water was deepening. There was no fog tonight and the beach was empty, other than the state birds that were already biting.

With no sign of her in either location, he stopped by Anna and Dave's to see if Madi was visiting with them. They were having supper, and said they hadn't seen her all day.

Josh went back to the cottage and tried her cell again. When he heard it ringing from inside the other room, he decided to sit outside on the patio and wait for her to return. *She must be on a walk,* he thought.

The flowers Lynne had arranged were on the iron table in front of him, and he stared at them while thinking about the week with Madi. How quickly things had unfolded from the first time they met. He thought of her standing there in her T-shirt and boxers. She had looked so amazing that he couldn't help staring at her. He remembered sitting at this very table and talking for hours the first night, gazing at the stars on the beach. The rest of the week was a whirlwind, beginning with the night at the lighthouse and making love for the first time. When she got back, he would be sure to tell her how incredible the week had been, and that he hoped they could still be a part of each other's lives after she returned to New York.

Josh had never felt this way about any woman before. Just the thought of looking into her almond-shaped eyes and kissing her wide, sexy mouth made him smile like a schoolboy. He would hate to think he would never see her again.

* * *

Where was the man in the wet suit taking her—and why? The farther they got offshore, the more she began to think he planned to dump her out at sea. How long could she swim, if at all, since her hands were tied behind her and she was gagged? The tears started to stream down her face as the reality of the situation seeped in.

She thought of her mother, whom she hadn't seen in years, busy enjoying her new life down south while Madi was wrapped up in her blossoming career. Madi wished she had made more of an effort to see her over the last few years. And there was Kristen, her best friend for so long. She would give anything to see her get married. Would she get the chance? As she cried silently, she prayed they would know how much she loved them.

It was smooth out here, and she looked at the reflection of the clouds on the water's surface. She watched the buoys float around her, and thought of the trip to the island with Josh. *She hadn't called him back.* Would he call again? Would he begin to worry, or would he think she was avoiding him and give up?

Please, Josh, don't give up on me.

CHAPTER SIXTEEN

He watched her back as he rowed. Her shoulders trembled and he knew she was crying. *She should be,* he thought. Another dirty whore, just like his mother and sister; she deserves to die as much as they had. By the time he finished with her, she'd be begging for forgiveness for all the sins she'd committed in his cottage.

Madi knew where they were going—Monroe Island—but instead of heading toward the familiar eastern shore, the man steered the kayak in the opposite direction, to the part of the island densely covered in woods. The dog, perched on the jump seat between she and the man, jumped out of the boat the first chance he had to leap to land. The man got out and pulled the kayak to shore, then grabbed her arm and pulled her out. She fell onto the embankment, landing unprotected on her stomach and cheek. He lifted her up roughly and grabbed her wrists, pushing her in front of him. He shoved her down on a large rock and then dragged the kayak to an overhang of foliage. It disappeared from sight.

They walked in silence through the woods until she saw the same building she and Josh had discovered, the one that looked like her boathouse. He unlocked the numerous padlocks on the door and pushed her inside, toward the bed, where she sat down clumsily. She was half sitting, half lying on her side. Her body began convulsing in fear as she anticipated the worst. The room was even more eerily identical to the boathouse on the inside, even down to the handmade shelves. She was on a single bed that mirrored the one she'd planned to sleep on one night, to enjoy the cool night air from the ocean. There would be no ocean breeze coming through this place, as they were buried in dense forest.

He was staring at her in disgust. Her tremors worsened as he approached.

Suddenly, they were interrupted by the dog, who bound into the cabin and jumped onto the bed next to Madi.

"You—out!" he ordered the dog, but the retriever didn't move. The man grabbed a shovel that was leaning against the would-be kitchen counter. Once more, he commanded the dog to get off the bed, this time with shovel raised. The dog sheepishly responded by slinking off and cowering at the foot of the bed. He still wouldn't leave Madi's side.

"Out," he shouted, kicking the dog in the haunches. The dog yelped and quickly disappeared out the front door.

Madi watched the man with frightened eyes. He moved about the one-room cabin, huffing and grunting with anger before turning to look at her. This time when he approached the bed, she began to cry, trying to plead with him from beneath the gag.

"Please," her muffled voice begged, "please . . . no."

He came closer, and as she got more emotional, he got

more agitated.

"Shut the fuck up, whore," he said, slapping her across the face.

She fell back on the bed and her head hit the wall. She tried to back herself into the corner as far from him as she could. He lunged toward her, reaching for her hair. She kicked him in the left leg as hard as she could. She had been aiming for his groin.

He laughed out loud. It was the most evil laugh she had ever heard.

"You bitch," he said as he grabbed hold of both her legs and tied them to the foot of the bed. She resisted with every ounce of her being. She tried to scream but it was useless. She was in the middle of nowhere with a lunatic who was going to kill her.

After he tied her down, he turned and went to the small counter near the door. He grabbed the gun he had placed there and walked out the front door.

She lay on the bed and sobbed, dreading his return.

* * *

It was eight o'clock and Josh was worried. He went back inside and looked in Madi's bags. There were items from the museum and some souvenir T-shirts. She had been in Rockland today. In her wallet, he found a receipt from the Black Bull Tavern. It was time-stamped 3:18 p.m., but it had two meals and two beverages on it. Who had she lunched with?

He crossed the lane and knocked on the neighbors' door.

"Sorry to bother you again, Dave, but could I come in?" Josh asked.

"Of course, come on in. Here, sit down. Would you like a drink?"

"No, thanks. Actually, I'm worried about Madi. She's still not home."

"Was she expecting you?" Dave asked.

"No, but I left her a couple of messages, and when she didn't call me back, I came by to surprise her by taking her out to dinner."

"Is her car there?"

"It is. And so are her purse, keys, and cell phone. I thought she might be at the beach, but it's dark now."

Anna heard them, and came in from the other room. "Does she have any friends in town, Josh?" she inquired.

"Not that I know of," he replied.

"Is it possible . . . you know . . . what happened to Kay?" she asked worriedly.

"No, Anna; I just booked Kay's ex-husband today. He's in jail."

"Oh, thank God," she said with a sigh of relief. "She's a very outgoing girl, Josh—maybe she's at another neighbor's house."

Josh remembered Madi saying that the man in the wet suit had told her he lived up the road. He asked Anna and Dave about it, and neither of them knew the man. But Anna had remembered seeing Madi with him the day she met her. They had been looking for sea glass together.

Josh agreed she was probably out socializing, and thanked them for their time. They asked that Josh let them know when he located her so they wouldn't worry. Josh promised, and headed up the lane. He climbed in the squad car and drove up the road slowly, examining each house on the street.

There were only five in total to the top of the lane, and two below Madi's cottage, and none of them were brown.

He radioed Dispatch to make sure there hadn't been any unusual calls or emergencies involving a young woman matching Madi's description. Nothing, he was told, but they would check the hospital and alert him if anything suspicious came in.

Was he was being paranoid, or had Madi just made a new friend?

He called Bellissimo and canceled his reservation before heading back to the lighthouse. He felt a wave of mixed emotions, ranging from disappointment to concern.

*   *   *

Josh saw a light on at the general store as he was passing by. Lynne must be cleaning up, he thought, as it was after closing time. He slowed when he saw the lights turn off, pulling over near the store. A minute later, Lynne emerged through the front door. He lowered the passenger window as Lynne walked over.

"Hey, Josh, what are you doing here?" she asked.

"Just heading home, and saw your light," Josh replied.

"What happened to the big date?" she asked as she peered into the car.

"I can't find her."

With a tilt of her head, Lynne asked, "What do you mean, can't find her?"

"She's not home. Don't know where she is. And, truthfully, I'm getting worried."

"Did you call her?"

"Yeah, I even stopped by. Her cell phone is at the cottage. So is her car."

"That's odd."

"I know."

"Josh, you might want to ask your mother if she knows where Madi might be," Lynne told him.

"My mother? Why on earth would she know?" he asked in surprise.

"They had lunch together," she informed him.

"What! Are you kidding me?" Josh remembered the receipt.

Lynne laughed. "No, I'm not."

"How? Why?" He was thoroughly confused, and dumbfounded that his mother had wiggled her way into his business.

"It was completely innocent, Josh," Lynne said, defending her friend. "Madi went to the museum today and they met each other. Then your mother happened to run into her at the Black Bull."

"Yeah, right," Josh retorted.

"I'm sure she didn't mean any harm. Maybe Madi told her what she was doing tonight."

"Or, maybe my mother kidnapped her and took her out gown shopping for our wedding." Josh didn't put anything past his mother.

With a loud laugh, Lynne wished him a good night and headed to her car.

He picked up his cell to dial, but immediately put it back on the seat and turned the car toward Rockland. It was time for a visit home to see his nosy mother. He was certain he would find Madi sitting at the dining room table, being bored to death with embarrassing photo albums of his childhood. He knew his mother would stop at absolutely nothing to find him a wife. She probably sweet-talked Madi into coming to the house for dinner, even going as far as picking Madi up at the cottage. As petrified as he was about what his mother might be saying to her, a flood of relief rushed over him at the idea of her being safe and sound.

* * *

The door opened and he entered the cabin without a word. He placed the gun behind the door, leaning it against the paneled wall, and turned to her. She was in the corner, just as he had left her. Still gagged and tied, she shrank back further when he glanced her way.

That pathetic dog had escaped him for now. He had missed with a single shot, and didn't want to risk a second being heard from the mainland or a passing boat. The dog would be back when he got hungry, and he'd take care of him then. He had grown tired of trying to train the dog, and besides, he didn't want to take him to the cottage. The only reason he had kept him this long was to warn him of trespassers to the island.

Now, what to do with this whore . . . He was still undecided. Should he throw her body into the ocean? If he disposed of her by water, he couldn't leave any marks on her body should she wash ashore. It would need to look like an accidental drowning. *What fun was that?*

Of course, he could just bury her on the island. No one would look for her out here. In fact, he could bury her and the dog together. He grabbed his lantern and a shovel and headed out into the night.

CHAPTER SEVENTEEN

Josh was the middle of five children—a true "middle child." He hadn't pursued the career his dad had wanted for him, and lately, all his mother seemed to care about was marrying him off, since at thirty-six, he was the only Daniels child without a ring on his left finger.

"I don't understand," she would tell her friends—in front of him, in fact. "He's so smart and handsome. Why can't he find a nice woman?"

"Hi, Dad." Josh greeted his father in the den off the garage. "You left your garage door open again."

His father grumbled something about the grandkids leaving it open, and quickly announced, "Your mother is in the kitchen."

This could only mean Josh was right; Madi must be in there with his mother. Why else would his father immediately direct him to the kitchen? *Oh, Lord.*

He strolled into the kitchen, trying to play it cool. His mother was sitting at her usual spot at the counter, reading glasses on and laptop open in front of her. Josh stopped, glanced around the room, and then back at his mother.

"Where is she?" he asked.

"Well, hello, Joshua! This is a lovely surprise. Where is who, honey?" she arose and planted a kiss on her son's cheek.

"You know who."

"I have no idea who you're talking about, sweetie."

"Madi."

"Ohhh, Madi," she replied with a tone that belied her innocent demeanor.

"Mom, I'm not joking around here," he insisted. "Where is she?"

"Honestly, Josh, I have no idea where that beautiful girl is. Why would you think she'd be here?"

"Lynne told me you had lunch with her today, and I thought maybe you'd hijacked her since I can't find her anywhere," he confessed, his disappointment apparent.

"I did have lunch with her. Of course, I didn't plan it—it just happened." As she tried to explain, she could see Josh wasn't buying it. "She's lovely, honey. We had a nice talk about you."

"Oh geez, Mom. Really?"

"Josh," she said, sudden concern in her voice, "what do you mean, you can't find her? Honey, are you pushing yourself too hard on that girl? You know, she's from New York City, and she's very worldly. You don't want to come on too strong or you'll chase her away. You—"

"Mom, stop," he interrupted. "I'm not chasing her—I'm worried about her."

He promptly retreated to the safety of the den. Dad was sitting in his recliner, watching *Law & Order*, episode 532.

I'll give him ten seconds before he solves the crime . . .

At that moment his mother came in and with one fell swoop grabbed the remote off his father's lap, sat next to Josh on the sofa, and turned off the television.

"What the hell are you doing, Judy? I was just about to solve it!" Josh's dad said.

"Ben, Joshua is worried about his girlfriend. He thinks she's missing." Turning toward Josh, she said, "My gosh, is the murderer still on the loose?"

"No, Mom, the murderer is not on the loose; we have him in custody. Madi and I sort of had a disagreement, so we didn't speak much today. I wanted to surprise her with dinner, but she's not at her rental house."

"The Walker cottage?" his mother asked.

"How did you . . . ?"

He stopped himself. Of course she knew where Madi was staying; they'd had lunch together. She probably knew Madi's whole life story, along with her plans for the future. She *was* champion of the inquisition, after all.

"Yes, the Walker cottage. Her car is there, but she's not. When Lynne told me you had lunch with her, I just assumed you had brought her back here to grill her some more."

"Josh, give your mother a little more credit than that," his father scolded. "They picked out the wedding invites in town, so there was no need to come back here," he said with a wink and a hearty chuckle. Josh did love his dad's laid-back sense of humor.

"Ben," Judy gave him a stern look.

Josh and his dad shared a laugh, while his mother scurried off to the kitchen, muttering "You two think you're sooo funny."

While Josh and his dad made small talk, Josh tried to reassure himself that Madi was okay. When they came back around to the subject of the "new girlfriend," Josh remembered that he'd wanted to ask his father about the Walker cottage.

"Madi went to the library and looked up the history of that old cottage."

"Oh yeah?" his dad asked, seemingly disinterested. By now, episode number 533 of *Law & Order* had begun.

"She mentioned that the Walkers left in 1962, and didn't leave a forwarding address," Josh said.

"No kidding," his dad said, quite aware of the recordkeeping in these small inlets, and the fact that everyone knew everything about each other.

"Wasn't Grandpa still fishing back then? Would he have known Walker?"

"Maybe," his dad said. "Why do you ask?"

"Madi's interested in the history of the cottage and who's owned it over the years. She's into that kind of thing," Josh explained.

"Your grandfather never forgets a name. He may not be able to tell you what he ate at his last meal, but he still remembers a lot of names from the past. The dementia hasn't taken everything away," his father said. "Why don't you stop by the nursing home and visit him tomorrow. He'd like that. You can ask if he knew Walker."

Josh took the hint, promising his dad he would visit his only remaining grandparent. Then he asked if there were any leftovers, as he was starving.

"Of course!" his mother shouted from the kitchen.

* * *

The tears wouldn't stop streaming down Madi's face. She heard the gunshot and assumed the man had shot his dog. She was still tied to the bed and it had been hours. She didn't know what time it was, but her stomach told her it was well past dinner. Wet-suit Man had taken a shovel and lantern, and his rifle. *That poor, sweet dog. He was just trying to protect her.*

She prayed that Josh would be concerned about her silence, but with Bill Andrews securely in jail, maybe he would just think she was ignoring him after their disagreement that morning.

Her arms were asleep behind her back and her ankles were raw from her attempts at pulling her feet free. She had to find a way out of this cabin and off this island; otherwise, her only way off would be in a body bag.

* * *

Madi was startled awake by the sound of Wet-Suit Man coming back into the cabin. She didn't know how much time had passed; she must have dozed off.

He pulled her roughly into a sitting position after removing her ankle restraints. Her feet tingled as she placed them on the floor. He removed her gag and warned her not to waste time trying to scream, because no one would hear her. She knew he was right. It was just the two of them on this deserted island. She shivered with fright and with the chill of the night air coming through the wallboards. He walked across the creaky, dusty floor and opened a can of beans. He stood with his back to her and inhaled the contents, using a rusty spoon.

She finally got up the courage to ask if she could use the bathroom, as she was bursting with discomfort. He threw the empty can and utensil into the tiny steel sink and moved toward her. He tied her ankles together again and followed her as she shuffled to the outhouse behind the cabin. She cried in relief when he untied her hands from behind her back, and she rubbed her wrists with vigor. There wasn't much of a chance she could escape out here in the cold black of the night. Even if she could, she doubted she'd be able to find her way back to the kayak, hidden in the brush.

Yet if she waited until morning, what would he do to her in the cabin tonight? She sat in the outhouse, weighing her options. She didn't want to see his face again, or his empty eyes. Maybe if she stayed in here and closed her eyes, this would all turn out to be nothing but a horrible nightmare.

No—you need to do something. Now.

He was pounding on the door, telling her to finish up and come out.

When she opened the door, he grabbed her left arm and yanked her out. She had managed to get the ankle ropes loose enough to rotate her body so she was facing him. She leaned forward, pretending to fall, and as her body rested flush against his, she placed a hand on each shoulder and kneed him in the groin with all her might. He went down hard.

She knew she had only moments before he would recover enough to grab her. She frantically pulled at the ropes on her ankles while he writhed in pain, cursing her like a madman. She almost had the ropes off when he half stood from his bent position and lunged for her, catching a chunk of her hair. She screamed as she felt the hair ripping from her scalp and hobbled sideways, tripping over an exposed root. Landing hard on her hip, she pulled the ropes free from her feet. She spun onto her knees and launched herself like a sprinter toward the woods.

* * *

She could hear him closing in behind her. She was weaving in and out, hoping to throw him off, but he was familiar with the terrain. She stumbled a few times, trying to muffle her cries. She would alternate between moving and hiding. Just when she thought she'd lost him, she could hear the brush crunching beneath his feet, or his breathing was so close, she was certain she could reach out and touch him. It was so dark under the canopy of trees. She needed to get to the rocky coast where the stars could light her way—although he'd be able to see her more easily in the clearing.

At the embankment, Madi could see the reflection of the faint stars in the surf beneath her. They sparkled like the string of white lights hung across the bow of the cottage. She had found her way to the side of the island where she and Josh had made love. *Would she ever see him again, and sit with him, laughing and drinking wine as the sun was setting?*

She would, she decided.

She could hardly see beyond the end of her nose, but she knew there was a steep descent to the giant, slippery rocks covered in live seaweed. She turned and dropped to her hands and knees to attempt to maneuver down the rocks. If she could climb her way across the rocks and over the center peak, she could hide on the other side and wait for a lobster boat to spot her in the morning.

By the time she heard his approach, it was too late.

He grabbed her just as she took her first step downward. She jerked away, only to free-fall directly onto the rock below. As her temple struck the rock, the last thing she saw was the incoming tide before she slipped into unconsciousness.

Turning his flashlight on her, he saw her body sprawled across a large, gray rock. She was facedown, her arm twisted in an unnatural way beneath her. As he moved the light up to her head, he saw blood emerging from her temple. He stood and watched for signs of life until he was convinced there weren't any.

The surf was now coming about three-quarters of the way up the stone embankment, and he knew it wouldn't be long before the entire area was submerged in high tide. She would be taken out to sea by morning. All he needed to do was set the kayak afloat. In just a matter of hours, this would be over, and the cottage would finally be his.

CHAPTER EIGHTEEN

After a sleepless night with no phone call from Madi, he headed toward the cottage on his way to the station. It was seven a.m., so he hoped he would find her sleeping. When no one answered his knock, he let himself in. The door was still unlocked, just as it had been the night before. He walked back to her bedroom, softly calling her name and hoping to see her buried under the white down comforter.

The bed was empty. The room looked just as it had yesterday evening. The purse, the bags, the cell phone—nothing had been moved.

He felt frantic. He picked up her cell phone to check the phone logs as he called for Dispatch on his radio.

"Dispatch. Go ahead, Sheriff."

"I have a missing person to report at Five Mahalas Lane. Please send a unit right away!"

"Ten-four, sir."

Then he dialed the last number she had called at three p.m. the day before.

* * *

"Hey, girl!" she answered happily.

"This is Sheriff Daniels from the Owls Head sheriff's department in Maine," Josh said. "With whom am I speaking?"

"Umm, this is Kristen Pearson. Are you the officer Madi told me about?" she asked playfully, and yet a little puzzled.

Surprised to hear she knew about him, he stumbled, "Why yes, I guess it is. And you are?"

"As a matter of fact, I'm her best friend. Don't tell me she hasn't mentioned me."

New Yorkers were so forward. And blunt. She caught him off guard, but only momentarily. "This is official police business. Not to alarm you, but can you tell me the context of your phone conversation with Madi yesterday afternoon, and whether you know her current whereabouts?"

"Whoa, buddy, what is this about? Why are you asking where Madi is? Don't you know?" she demanded. "What's happening?"

"Miss Pearson, I have reason to believe Madi may be missing."

"Oh my God! She told me about the murders. Oh my God!"

"Calm down, please," he said. "The murder suspect is behind bars. I need to know if she told you where she was going last night," he persisted.

"No, she didn't. She simply talked about meeting you, and said that she was having a good time, despite the chaos that was going on next door," she explained. "Can you please tell me what makes you think she's missing? I'm sort of freaking out here."

Josh told her the story he'd told his parents the night before, adding that Madi's things had remained untouched in the cottage overnight.

"I haven't known Madi very long, but it's unusual to me that she would leave her purse and cell phone home all night," Josh said. "Something just doesn't feel right."

"I agree; something is really wrong. You need to find her!" Kristen implored. "I'm on my way up there. I can't stay here knowing she's missing. I'll be there in seven or eight hours, depending on traffic."

Josh gave Kristen the address of the cottage for her GPS, and they made tentative plans to meet upon her arrival. Then she gathered a few essential items and left her apartment, dashing down the stairs to run the five blocks to the garage where her car was stored.

After hanging up with Kristen, Josh sat in the cottage for a few minutes, contemplating Madi's confusion between the man in the wet suit and Andrews. He needed to find out who this mysterious man was, and if Madi is with him. When Madi had mentioned his eyes, she sounded frightened. He would never forgive himself if this man has done anything to harm her.

* * *

While his team was searching in and around the Walker cottage for clues pertaining to Madi's whereabouts, Josh headed to Camden Hills Assisted Living Center to pay his grandfather a visit. Madi had said that the man in the wet suit had grown up on Mahalas Lane, and he was hoping his grandfather might remember some of the former residents—including, possibly, this particular man. If Madi was with him, Josh had to find out who he is. It was a long shot, but Josh needed to try.

He signed in, and the nurse told him his grandfather was in his room.

"Hi, Grandpa, it's Joshua—your grandson," he said when he walked in. "Judy and Ben's son."

Josh never knew who he would find when he arrived at the nursing home facility—the engaging, sharp-witted man who had spent his life at sea, or the withered old man who didn't know your name or face. It was always a bittersweet experience—part of the reason Josh tried to avoid these visits.

The nursing home was decorated like a four-star hotel. His grandfather spent most of his days in the common room, staring into space or bickering with other residents over whose sofa was whose. Josh wheeled him down there now to try and gather what information he could about the past residents of Mahalas Lane.

Grandpa had only been here a few years, since his fall. He was ninety-two, and had lived on his own until he'd slipped off a curb and broken his hip. Two surgeries later, his mind seemed to have deteriorated as quickly as his body. Just this past Christmas, he'd been sentenced to a wheelchair because his bones were so brittle.

In his heyday, Marcus Daniels was captain of the *Katherine*, and made a name for himself as one of the best fishermen in the area. He was an avid storyteller, and entertained Josh as a child with tales of his life out on the water.

"Grandpa, do you remember Thomas Walker?" he asked.

"That bastard! Sure do," he replied.

"Really? You knew him?" Josh played along, anxious to learn something meaningful.

"Yup, he was on one of my crews. One of my best fishermen."

"Why did you call him a bastard, then, Grandpa?" Josh asked, still unsure if his grandfather was having a moment of lucidity or not.

"He stole my girl," he said with a chuckle. "Ahh, not really; I dated her briefly. But I always gave him a hard time about it, even on the day of their wedding. I officiated," he recalled fondly.

Josh couldn't believe his ears. Was this real, or just another tall tale? During some visits his grandfather was convinced the nurses were trying to smother him with his own pillow.

"What was his wife's name, Grandpa?"

"Margaret, it was. Lovely Margaret . . . such a tragic end."

"Why tragic?" asked Josh.

"Because that crazy son of theirs murdered them, that's why! Such a shame . . ." Josh saw his grandfather tear up and then start to sob. This was not a good sign. Grandpa had become quite depressed in the home, and the family tried desperately not to upset him. Any little episode could result in days of confusion.

"No, Grandpa, I'm sure that's not what happened to your friends. They moved, I think. In fact, I'm sure of it. It says so in the library records," Josh insisted, hoping to keep him from checking out of the conversation. *Another murder?* Josh thought. *This can't be true.*

"Joshua," his grandpa said, looking clearly into his eyes and leaning forward in his chair, "that's just the story we told everyone back then so as not to create a panic on the peninsula, and to keep the other seamen's families at peace while we were gone. They locked the kid up in a mental institution where he belonged, and sent the sister off to boarding school. Now, don't tell anyone, okay, boy?"

Lord have mercy. What kind of place was Owls Head? Was it not the safe, peaceful town Josh knew after all?

"Grandpa, what was the name of the hospital—do you remember?"

"What hospital?" His grandfather now looked confused.

"The one where Thomas Walker's son was sent."

"I don't know any Thomas Walker. Who's he? Where's my nurse . . . I need to piss. Who are you? Get out!"

* * *

Madi felt cold and damp as she slipped in and out of consciousness. She could feel his breathing above her, so close she wished she was dead already. *He had found her.* Her head throbbed and she was dizzy. The weight of his body was warm. It repulsed her.

She moved her head to the right to vomit, feeling her will to live leave her body along with the bile she choked up. She slipped away again.

Please God, she prayed, *take me now and let this be over.*

* * *

The assisted living center was located just north of the center of Camden, a wealthy waterfront village two towns north of Rockland. It was on the west side of Route One, the road that ran along the Maine coast from Massachusetts all the way north to New Brunswick, Canada. Between the facility and the village was the entrance to Camden Hills State Park, a 5,700-acre parcel with over thirty miles of hiking trails. At its peak, Mount Battie overlooked Camden Harbor and dozens of islands off the coast. Josh had been to the top many times growing up, and it was one of his favorite places.

His grandfather used to take him up the circular staircase of the stone lookout tower and tell him stories of how his own father had helped the government to build the park back in the 1930s. As he listened to his grandfather, he would study the sailboats dotting Penobscot Bay and try to pinpoint Cadillac Mountain at Acadia National Park, nearly a hundred miles away in Bar Harbor. Josh remembered the piece of quartzite he used to carry around in his pocket that his grandfather once chipped off Mount Battie and gave to him, telling him how the mineral was hundreds of years old.

As he raced past the entrance to the park, he called Kristen to see how far she had gotten. It would take him nearly an hour in the daytime traffic through the towns of Camden, Rockport, and Rockland to get back to Madi's cottage. He would try to cut that in half using his lights and siren. He told Kristen he would meet her there later, assuring her that a patrol car would be guarding the entrance to the lane, and the officer would let her pass. First, he would head to the University College of Rockland library to find out the names of all the mental hospitals in Maine back in the 1960s. He needed to know what had become of Tom and Margaret Walker's children.

On his way, he put out an all-points bulletin for a six-foot-tall man in his late fifties, salt-and-pepper hair, with dark eyes. No, he explained to Dispatch, not Bill Andrews—another man fitting the same description. He instructed them to secure the perimeter of Mahalas Lane and all roads exiting Owls Head.

"What was he wearing?" Dispatch asked.

"A wet suit," Josh replied.

CHAPTER NINETEEN

After he checked the rocks and saw that the woman's body was gone, he was satisfied that she had been taken out by the tide. It had been a windy day prior, and he knew the strong gusts would add to the tidal current. On days like yesterday, the tide could easily reach eleven feet on that part of the island. The rings around the lobster buoys had also given him an indication of the strength of the current. It had been over eight hours since she'd fallen—ample time for the tide to reach its highest point and retreat back to sea. She might easily have been pulled from shore a good two or three hours ago.

He maneuvered around the opposite side of the island to the covered spot where he'd hidden the kayak. He set it adrift and headed back to camp. With no sign of the dog and no barking to speak of, he deduced that he had, in fact, hit him the night before with the rifle. He began his work of locking up the cabin for an extended period, since he would no longer need to live out here.

He was going home.

* * *

Within an hour, Josh had located the names of five hospitals that had treated the criminally insane in the 1960s. He had his investigator working on finding the social security numbers of the Walker children, their last known whereabouts, and whether one of them had been treated at a mental institution in the past thirty years. While he waited, he drove back to Mahalas Lane to try and find this wet-suit man living in the nonexistent brown house.

It didn't take long for Josh to visit, interrogate, and virtually terrify every resident on the lane. By the third of the seven houses surrounding the cottage, his patience had eroded, and he was getting angrier with each unanswered question. And the more he replayed his last conversation with Madi, the guiltier he felt about her disappearance.

His eyes, Josh. The man in the wet suit and the man in the window have the same eyes. I swear they are one and the same. She had pleaded with him to believe her, but because he had chased Bill Andrews out of town, Josh had dismissed her fear of the man in the wet suit. He was sure her dream was jumbled from all the activities of the week.

But what if Madi was right about who she had seen through the window the other night? Why would the man in the wet suit be lurking outside the cottage? What if Bill Andrews *hadn't* been the one to kill his ex-wife after all, and there was a murderer still at large? He thought of Andrews's look of surprise when Josh had told him Kay was dead.

All he knew now was that he had to find Madi. If there was a killer on the loose, she was in great danger.

*   *   *

Kristen arrived at the rental cottage at quarter past three that afternoon. Their meeting was as awkward as any Josh had ever experienced. He shook her hand and introduced himself as Josh, and she looked at him like he had just about killed her best friend with his bare hands.

"Where is she, Sheriff? What have you found out so far?" Kristen grilled him about every moment, every conversation, and every detail of their time together. He answered meekly and methodically, and by the end of nearly an hour, Kristen knew everything there was to know about Madi and Josh's week together, as well as the murder investigations and Madi's suspicion over the man in the wet suit.

They agreed that Kristen would stay at the cottage while Josh went to the department to get the results of the Walker research, hoping to learn if his grandfather's claims were true, and to determine where the Walkers' son might be now.

The officers had found nothing of interest among Madi's things, and had moved on to the surrounding woods and shoreline to continue their hunt. Kristen was hopeful she might find something that would give them a clue—a phone call, a receipt, something unusual that only Madi's best friend would recognize.

She started in Madi's bedroom, stopping for a minute to sit on the bed. The pillows smelled like Madi . . .

Memories of their long friendship flowed through her mind. She had shared so much of her life with Madi . . . school, boyfriends, ups and downs in their careers. Madi was the first person she had told of her upcoming nuptials; she'd asked her to be her maid of honor. She was her best friend in the world. She couldn't imagine her life without Madi in it. Where could she be?

* * *

A member of the Coast Guard called Josh just as he was arriving at his office.

"A kayak?" Josh repeated. "And no one was in it? What about clothes—belongings?"

His heart sank as he listened. The water temperature was 38 degrees, the coast guardsman explained. If the kayak had capsized, Madi wouldn't have been able to survive for long in the icy water. They would begin a search of the surrounding coastal islands, but there were over a hundred. Word had gotten out that the missing woman was personally connected to the sheriff, so the caller was sensitive with his choice of words.

"I'm very sorry, Sheriff—the odds are very slim for finding her alive. We will make every effort, sir."

Josh ended the call and stared out the window of his squad car. He was frozen with disbelief, shock, horror . . . and confusion. Madi's rental kayak was still on the boathouse deck, he had checked the day before. Had she been kayaking with this man? Had they both capsized?

* * *

Kristen came across the journal in Madi's room during her search for clues, and quickly skimmed through some of the entries. She felt like she was reading a novel. The cottage, the murdered parents . . . Sarah, the sister, returning to Owls Head to buy back her childhood home . . . the crazy brother who had wanted to move in with her . . . Sarah, frightened of him. And then the journal ended.

"Oh my God!" Kristen cried aloud. Here it was, right in front of her: proof that Josh's grandfather had spoken the truth.

Could Sarah's brother be this man in the wet suit?

Kristen immediately dialed Josh and jumped up to grab her shoes and keys from the bedroom. She had to tell Josh what she'd just read, and she needed to get out of this house before she, too, went missing.

Josh was on his way back to the cottage when his cell phone rang. It was Kristen. He didn't know if he could get out the words to tell her about the deserted kayak.

"Hello?" he answered quietly.

He heard a scuffle and a gasp, and then the phone went dead.

Josh hit the sirens, called for backup, and accelerated toward the cottage.

* * *

Madi was having her favorite dream again. The Adirondack chairs, the perfect house with the wraparound porch, the kids running around in the yard, and Josh. He was smiling at her while he played catch with their son. She inhaled deeply through her nose and the cold, dank smell of the ground beneath her rushed in.

She was in a shallow grave. Her dream wasn't real; instead, she was in her own personal nightmare. She was dying. *Or was she already dead?* If she was, she prayed for God to come and take her soul off this hideous island.

She could hear him breathing next to her. Her body was aching and numb. He had beaten her, she was certain, and perhaps raped her as well. She felt like she'd been run over by a Mack truck.

Please, God, let it end.

* * *

Josh and his deputies kicked the cottage door open, guns drawn. The man was standing there, waiting . . . smiling. The look of terror on Kristen's face said it all, as did the butcher knife the man was holding to her neck. The afternoon sun streaming through the side window reflected off the blade.

Madi had been wary of a man in the neighborhood, and had even thought it could have been Andrews. But this definitely wasn't the lobsterman he had arrested just the night before. Was this the man in the wet suit Madi had talked about? And if so, what had he done with her?

These thoughts ran wild through his head in the few seconds he stood there, his gun pointing at the man.

"Drop the knife," Josh commanded.

"I will kill her too," the man flatly announced.

"I said, drop it. Or I'll shoot."

Kristen squirmed and squealed as he held his hand firmly over her mouth.

"This is my house, and no whore bitch will ever take it from me again," the man declared. He pressed the knife into Kristen's throat.

At that moment, Josh closed his left eye and pulled the

trigger. The bullet hit the man squarely between the eyes and he collapsed to the ground.

Kristen screamed and pulled herself away, running toward Josh. He grabbed her and they sank to the floor. Kristen sobbed in Josh's arms as his officers moved in.

After checking Kristen's neck and seeing it was only a flesh wound, he lead her to Madi's bedroom to await the paramedics. He moistened a washcloth from the main floor bathroom, and wiped the victim's blood splatters from Kristen's face, while trying to calm her down. When the ambulance arrived, Josh returned to the living room where the man, presumably Walker, was pronounced dead. Josh was beside himself. He called in emergency search teams from Camden to Thomaston and assigned each of his own officers an area of the peninsula. Then he called every officer in his department to duty. He wouldn't rest until he found Madi's body.

After bandaging her up, the paramedics insisted on taking Kristen to the Rockland Medical Center for a closer evaluation. At first, she didn't want to leave the cottage, where she felt closest to her missing friend, but eventually she agreed to go to the hospital. Later that evening, when she was cleared by the attending doctor, an officer took Kristen to the light keeper's cottage and stayed with her until Josh would return from searching for Madi.

CHAPTER TWENTY

Although the sky outside was lit up by constellations as bright as a ship's fleet, it was the darkest night of Joshua Daniels's life. It was nearly four in the morning and while he was emotionally and physically exhausted, he could not sleep a wink. He lay on the sofa, recounting the steps that had led to this disastrous outcome. The department had tracked down the whereabouts of the Walker children and it was confirmed: The man he'd shot earlier had in fact been the troubled son of Thomas and Margaret Walker.

Sarah Walker's social security number was traced to one Sarah Wilson, the former owner of the cottage. There was no doubt in his mind that Sarah's "accidental death" had been caused by her sociopathic brother. And the cabin on Monroe Island seemed to be no coincidence either. They believed Thomas Jr. had built it when he was released from the hospital.

Every once in a while he could hear Kristen's muffled sobs through the wall of his bedroom, which he had insisted she take so she could get some sleep. She would be leaving in the morning to return to New York, to assist in planning her best friend's memorial service. Of course, no actual funeral would take place, since no body had been retrieved from the frigid waters of Penobscot Bay.

Madi's mother had been notified. He had insisted that he make the call rather than Kristen. It was the least he could do, considering he felt completely responsible for Madi's death at the hands of Thomas Walker Jr. The eleven o'clock news made him out to be some kind of hero for capturing not just one, but two, murderers. He knew the truth, though; he was nothing of the sort.

Josh had never believed in love at first sight until Madi came along. A plaque in his parents' bedroom was inscribed with the French phrase, *Coup de foudre*. It meant "love at first sight." He was certain he had been a willing victim of this with Madi . . . as sure as he was that he had failed her when she'd needed him most. Had he listened to Madi's fears about the man in the wet suit, she would be alive right now. He wasn't sure how he was going to live with that knowledge, or how he was going to live without her.

He wasn't sure how he was going to live. Period.

* * *

It was shortly after dawn when Josh got another call from the Coast Guard. The divers had stopped their search the previous evening, planning to resume at first light. A crime scene investigator from Portland had been brought in late the night before for debriefing, and was to lead a thorough search of Monroe Island and the cabin. He would attempt to determine whether Madi had been sexually assaulted, beaten, or killed at the cabin prior to being dumped at sea.

"Talk to me," a puffy-eyed Josh commanded.

"Sheriff, we have located a woman buried on Monroe Island. We have reason to believe it's Madi Lyons."

"*Buried?*" Josh choked back tears as he softly repeated the word, dreading the permanence of her loss. *So there it was.* His heart sank so deep he was sure it was buried far beneath Madi's body. He was overtaken by grief and barely heard the caller's next words.

"Yes, Sheriff, in a shallow grave. She's alive—but barely."

What! Did he say alive?

"Repeat, Officer."

The man repeated his report, and Josh felt a surge of joy.

A medical helicopter was on its way to pick up Josh at the regional airfield—the same one that had caused such a ruckus among residents regarding its expansion, and subsequent increased commercial flights. Until recently, such trivial topics were the only signs of strife in this sleepy Maine town. Those days seemed so long ago, and so unimportant now.

* * *

Josh could see the clearing below as they landed, and looked out at a team of coast guardsmen waving to them. Oddly, standing next to them was a dog. *The same stray dog that Madi was so fond of.* Josh was a ball of anxiety, and at moments during the flight had actually held his breath for so long he'd felt faint.

He and the medic jumped out of the helicopter, and the officers led them into the woods. As they hurriedly weaved through the brush, they explained that when they were circling the island, the golden retriever had run along the shore, barking frantically at them. Normally, they would have assumed that someone was picnicking with their dog, not uncommon on these unpopulated islands. However, it was rare to see someone out there so early in the morning.

The dog was going ballistic, spinning and jumping like mad. Once they had come ashore, the dog had barked at them to follow him. He led them to a shallow grave where they had found her.

Along with the medic, Josh crawled through the underbrush with flashlight in hand. The two men found a roughly dug trough in the ground, protected by the surrounding bushes and branches. The dog had clearly prepared the area in an effort to protect Madi from the elements. It wasn't big enough for the two men, so they crawled in single file alongside Madi.

She was unconscious, her breathing so shallow it was hardly audible. She was cold to the touch and had a large wound on her right temple. While her hair was matted with blood, the wound itself was clean. She looked the color of death, an opaque pallid blue like the people in the movie *Zombies*. Josh had seen it before, both in his Academy training, and among drug overdose cases at the morgue.

The medic looked at Josh and said softly, amazement in his voice, "The dog licked her wound clean."

"Can you save her?"

"I will do my best, sir. I'm going to need some room."

Against his will, Josh retreated from the crawl space. Outside, Josh paced back and forth, and prayed for what seemed like an eternity.

Finally, the medic stabilized Madi enough to move her, and with the help of the other officers, got her onto a portable gurney outside of the cramped space. They hooked her up to IV fluids, covered her in blankets, bandaged her head wound, and set her broken arm in a temporary brace. She was still unconscious.

"Her body temperature is very low, and she's severely dehydrated," the medic told Josh. "She has a concussion and some broken bones and ribs. It will be touch and go for a while with the hypothermia, but I think she'll pull through."

Josh felt a wave of relief and happiness that he had never experienced before. If he hadn't already been certain this woman was meant to be in his life, there was no longer any doubt. He couldn't live a day in this world without her. He had to let her know.

"Madi," he said, squeezing her cold, limp hand with his, "I have looked for you my whole life, and I would have continued to look for you forever. I found you twice now, and I'm never going to let you go." Then he leaned down and whispered in her ear. "Do you hear me, Madelyn DeLeone? I need you. I love you. Please don't leave me here alone."

He couldn't be sure, but he thought he felt her squeeze him back.

CHAPTER TWENTY ONE

"Please, Madi. Make me the luckiest man alive and marry me."

She was overcome with emotion as he opened the tiny velvet box he had pulled from his pocket. *Who was the lucky one?* she thought, as her eyes darted from the stunning solitaire ring to Josh's tear-streaked face. The man kneeling in front of her hadn't left her side in weeks. First, his bedside vigil at the hospital, and then, this past week, doting on her as she regained her strength at the light keeper's cottage.

It was their first night out since she had been released from the hospital. Josh insisted on taking her to Bellissimo as soon as she was up to it, for the romantic dinner he had planned before her ordeal.

From the moment she regained consciousness and saw Josh's relieved face smiling at her, everything changed for Madi.

She had had it all wrong. She knew now that her life would never be complete without love, regardless of the level of success she achieved in her career. She loved this man with all her heart and soul. There was no doubt she had been put on this planet, and this peninsula, to meet Josh.

"Madi?" he asked, interrupting her thoughts.

"Yes," she gushed. "Of course I'll marry you!"

* * *

Just as the trees were shedding their final autumnal leaves, a light was finally shed on the tragedies that had befallen their tight-knit community this past summer. Bill Andrews was convicted of the murder of line cook Robert Peterson and sent to prison. The indictment against him for the murder of his ex-wife was dropped, for lack of evidence.

The local media reported that they had few details, but a man named Thomas Walker Jr., a former resident of 5 Mahalas Lane, had murdered his parents in their home during a fit of rage in 1962. And, while not confirmed by authorities, there was speculation that he had also killed two Mahalas Lane residents: Sarah Wilson, his sister, and Kay Andrews. Walker's motives were still unclear, but he had been gunned-down by authorities in the midst of his attempted abduction of Kristen Pearson.

Josh and Madi knew the connection, as did Andrews's defense attorney and the state's attorney's office. Walker had come back to Owls Head to claim his childhood home, murdering his sister to do so. The best conclusion they could reach regarding his reason for killing Kay was that he might have believed Sarah told Kay about her family's dark secret.

CHAPTER TWENTY TWO

The handkerchief over Josh's eyes made him feel completely helpless and foolish. Regardless, he played along, knowing how important this was to her.

Madi guided him through the cold streets of Rockland to a spot he had spent many of his days off this past winter. However, she wouldn't let him go near the location this past week so she could put the finishing touches on it. He'd even had to pinky-promise that he wouldn't drive that direction through town.

"Okay, are you ready?" Madi asked him, sounding like a child at Christmas.

"Ready!" he replied with enthusiasm.

At that, she untied Josh's blindfold. Right next door to their favorite bookstore and café, there was a new business in town. There, on the glass storefront, the prettiest words he had ever seen: MADELYN DANIELS MARKETING.

In the reflection he saw himself and his wife, who was beaming from ear to ear. Inside, lying on a huge plaid bed in the small office lobby was the golden retriever who had saved her life. They had named him Spot, after the legendary lighthouse canine, despite the fact that his wavy red coat had not a single spot. To this day, they weren't sure exactly how the dog had managed to get Madi from the rocks on the north side of island around to the wooded cover of the crawl space he'd dug. Her doctors suggested she most likely had gone in and out of consciousness and that Spot had led her to safety.

Madi didn't remember a thing after she fell—only bits and pieces of dreams and nightmares. She faintly recalled somebody lying on top of her, and they believed it must have been the dog, keeping her warm. The doctors said she may or may not get her memory back of what actually occurred. She and Josh were just fine with that; they wanted to put it all behind them and forget about lunatic sons of sailors and crazy ex-husbands.

With one killer dead and one in prison for the murder of Kay's lover, Owls Head had returned to the peaceful Maine town it had been before the arrival of Madi Lyons. The chatter about the Walker cottage and the gruesome actions of the deranged son had waned over the past months, and would someday become another of the legends of Owls Head, along with stories of haunted lighthouses and heroic dogs named Spot.

"C'mon, let me show you inside!" Madi pulled Josh through the front door and excitedly showed him all the furnishings and decor she had purchased at the two antiques shops in the village.

"Here's my desk, and here's a table to meet with clients, and over here . . ."

As she showed him every lamp, every picture, every detail

of her new office, he marveled at her and the pure joy she was exuding. She had already added her feminine touch to the light keeper's cottage, making it a warm and cozy home for them. They wasted no time getting married, quickly arranging a small ceremony and intimate celebration with Kristen and each of their families at Josh's parents' house before summer had ended. Madi's mom and husband had driven up for it and Kristen flew back in for the weekend to stand by her best friend's side.

These recent months had been the best of his life, and he was happy that Madi was pursuing her passion with this new venture. She was so beautiful, showing off her office with her wild Italian hands flying about . . . He particularly loved it when she paused to place them atop her growing belly.

Josh was in heaven, knowing he would soon become a father to their little baby boy.

PART TWO

EIGHT YEARS LATER

Chapter Twenty Three

Madi couldn't believe Noah was turning eight today. While she blew up balloons and strung royal blue streamers across the living room ceiling, the previous seven birthday parties replayed in her mind, one by one. He had been such a good baby, very content. He was a good eater, too—just like his daddy, Judy always said.

She heard Spot bark at the beep of the mailman's horn as he pulled up the lighthouse's long drive. She opened the front door and let Spot out, and he ran to retrieve the mail from the carrier, delivering it right to Madi's hands. She waved to the familiar mailman as she closed the front door behind her beloved companion. Along with the usual junk mail were a few more birthday cards for Noah, from friends and family back in New York.

"Noah," she called down the hall to her son's room. "You've got more mail."

"I'm coming!" he yelled back, excitement in his voice.

Arriving in a matter of seconds, he asked excitedly, "Do

they have money in them?"

"I don't know," she said. "You really shouldn't expect it, sweetheart; that's not polite."

"But I need twenty more dollars to get that remote-control sailboat at Curry's. I want to sail it in the bay this weekend when Aunt Kristen gets here."

Madi shook her head and went back to the business of decorating. She, too, couldn't wait until Kristen, John, and Max arrived in three days. She hadn't seen them since last summer, and Max was almost four now. He was probably huge. She'd been so glad to hear they were coming for Easter this year, and so close to Noah's birthday.

Her son's school friends would be here at four o'clock. She had one hour to get the house ready for ten rowdy third graders. It was a good thing she was taking the following week off to spend time with Kris. She was in need of a break from the office. Madelyn Daniels Marketing had been amazingly busy as of late. With her recent acquisition of the Knox County tourism account, she'd been working practically around the clock.

Thank goodness for Josh, and the fact that his job was relatively quiet these days. Sure, there had been some months of mayhem after Josh had shot Thomas Walker Jr., but that was many years ago, and things had long since returned to normal. He always did a great job helping Madi around the house and with their son. It was a relief to have such a supportive husband, as she'd been putting in some very late nights at the office in Rockland. She loved every second of it, but missed the time at home with her guys.

"Mom, I got it! Aunt Caryn sent me fifty dollars! Can we go to the store? Please, please?" he begged. Caryn was Madi's favorite cousin from New Jersey.

"We don't have time today; your party is starting soon. Tomorrow after school, I promise," she replied.

With a little pout, he went back to opening cards, tearing the envelopes carelessly and piling his loot on the kitchen table.

"What the heck?" he asked in disgust, slapping down one of the pieces of mail on the table.

"Young man, we don't talk like that," she scolded. "And I told you, it's impolite to expect money."

"It doesn't even have a name on it, Mom," he announced.

"Really? Did someone forget to sign it? What does it say, honey?" she asked.

He read the handwriting inside the card. "It just says, 'It's mine.'"

Madi froze on the folding chair she was perched on and dropped the roll of streamers to the ground. Stepping down, she felt the room spin and reached for the side of the sofa just as she fainted.

* * *

Josh had been on his way home for the party when his son called in a panic.

"Mommy fell off the chair and passed out!" he cried.

"Okay, Noah, stay calm. I'm almost there. Listen, buddy, I need you to put your hand in front of Mommy's mouth and tell me if you can feel her breath," Josh instructed in the calm and collected manner in which he was trained to handle emergencies.

"Yes, Dad, I can!" he replied with relief.

"Good, son. Now gently pat her on the cheek and call

her name."

"Mom, wake up. Mama, please wake up."

Josh could hear his son softly coaxing his wife awake.

"Okay, Dad, she's starting to open her eyes," Noah reported happily.

"I'm almost to the driveway. I'll be right there, son," Josh said as he sped through the park.

Madi had mentioned feeling light-headed for the past week or two, and Josh had urged her to go to the doctor. "I don't have time to go to the doctor" was always her response. Her workload was overwhelming, and it was clearly taking a toll on her. When he expressed his concern, she just said, "I'm fine. Just stressed out from work, that's all. I probably forgot to eat."

When Josh got inside, he checked Madi out further and was ultimately convinced she was all right—though he did insist she make an appointment with the doctor for the following week, after Kristen left.

Madi had just enough time before the party guests arrived to tell Josh about the strange message that had come in the mail.

"What do you think this is, Josh? Some kind of joke?"

"Who would do that?" he replied, even though they both had a pretty good idea.

They decided to get through the party as best they could, for Noah's sake, and to discuss it further after all the kids had gone home.

Madi asked Kendyl, one of the moms, to take Noah home with her for the night so she and Josh could talk freely, without their son overhearing them. She took Kendyl into the bathroom and showed her the card Noah had received.

Kendyl said she'd be glad to help in any way she could.

Kendyl knew the history of Josh and Madi's relationship, and was just as concerned about the note as they were. The boys were beyond thrilled about their surprise sleepover, especially since it was a school night, when such things were usually not allowed.

Kendyl's son Grayson and Noah were lifelong buddies. They'd known each other since birth and were inseparable. Madi and Kendyl had met while they were delivering their children. The two women were suite mates in the maternity ward at Rockport's Pen Bay Medical Center. If asked how they had become such good friends, they always explained that when you share the first few hours of your child's life with someone, you form a bond that can't be broken.

Kendyl was one of Madi's best friends in Maine. There were two others that qualified as well. The Core, they called themselves, made up of Madi, Kendyl, Michaela, and Valerie. Madi had met and become friends with each of them separately, but they eventually came together as a group. They had grown to adore each other. Michaela was Madi's banker, and Valerie was a media buyer for one of her clients. Every first Thursday night of the month, they converged in Madi's office as founding members of the Midcoast Book Club.

At one point, they had considered changing the name of their group to the Midcoast Book & Wine Club, or, better yet, the Midcoast Wine Club, because over the years it had taken on more of a girls'-night-out feel. They would sit on the worn leather sofas in Madi's lobby for hours, chatting about their lives, their relationships with their husbands, their kids, their favorite reality shows, and pretty much everything else under the sun. Most months, one or more of them hadn't had the time to finish the assigned reading, so the actual literary discussion was usually short-lived. On top of that, Kendyl simply refused to read any of the books, claiming "I don't read unless it has pictures," which always gave the ladies a good laugh. Admittedly, she was only there for the wine, the gossip, and the camaraderie.

Madi felt so blessed to be living this life. She had a devoted husband, a wonderful son, and great friends in Maine. As insane as it sounded, she was grateful to Thomas Walker Jr. and Bill Andrews. If it weren't for them, she wouldn't have met Josh, and she certainly wouldn't have given up her life in New York City to live in rural Maine. She believed that it had all happened for a reason—so she could find her destiny here with Josh.

Things between she and her husband had never been better. A day hadn't passed without Josh telling her how lucky he was to have found her. And she was more in love with her soul mate than ever. All it took was one look into those crystal blue eyes, and she would melt, every time.

* * *

Josh held open the door to the sheriff's department and Madi stepped inside.

"Hi, Em," Madi greeted the officer at the desk.

"Hey there, you two. How was the party?" Emily asked with a contagious smile.

"It was great. All the boys had a good time," Madi replied.

"So," Emily said, straining her neck to look behind Josh, "where's the birthday boy? Did you bring him to see me?"

Josh answered this time. "He's not with us, actually. He's sleeping over at Grayson's."

"Really . . ." Emily paused. "Let me get this straight: The two of you have a night alone and you brought Madi here, Josh? You're hopeless. Have I taught you nothing?"

Her humor didn't elicit the expected response, and Madi didn't join her in their typical shared routine of razzing Josh. Emily looked at each of them for a moment and asked, "Okay, what gives?"

Madi reached in her purse and handed Emily the card with the cryptic message.

"What the fu—dgggge?" Emily caught herself, having vowed to give up cursing for Lent. The other officers had bets on how soon she would slip up, since she was known to curse like a sailor.

Emily knew everything there was to know about the past events in Owls Head. In fact, she'd been on the force when the Walker/Andrews case had been open. She and Josh had gone to the Police Academy together, and until recent months, Emily was Josh's partner on the road. Since finding out she was pregnant, Josh had ordered her to Dispatch. The desk assignment had been seconded by her doctor, and she was not at all happy with it, letting Josh know every chance she got. Josh ignored her continued pleas to return to active duty, as she was over forty with this pregnancy, and her blood pressure was erratic.

"Em, I'm going to grab the files on the Walker/Andrews case and take them home. Can you call the Maine State Prison and get me a meeting with Andrews? I'm going to pay him a visit and find out if he's up to his old tricks again."

"Sure thing, boss," Emily replied, adding casually, "I'll go with you."

Josh raised his eyebrows at his partner and friend, which she clearly understood as his unspoken *No*.

* * *

Madi and Josh pulled into their driveway at just past eight p.m. Madi was starving, and luckily they'd caught Lynne just before she locked up the general store for the night. She made them a couple quick burgers to go, and after hearing about the card, she promised not to tell Judy. She knew Josh's mother would worry herself sick over it. Madi was keenly aware that her husband was a target for potential retaliation from felons he had arrested. It was part of the job, a fact she had come to accept. Most of the threats he had received in the past were idle ones, and they learned to be cautious without living in fear.

She called from the front steps for Spot to come inside. He spent most of his evenings roaming the section of the park at the base of the lighthouse. He was truly an outdoor dog, and an extremely good guard dog as well, much like his lighthouse namesake. Thankfully, it had been a mild winter, and she was able to let him go outdoors much earlier than usual this year.

When he didn't come after the third call, Josh put his jacket back on and went out to find him. Some nights the retriever would wander a bit far, especially when the moon was full and the tide gave him a runway on the beach located on the north side of the lighthouse. It was dark maneuvering down the wooded area behind the house, but Josh knew his way. When he came out onto the clearing of lawn above the sandy beach, he saw Spot down below, lying on the beach.

"Spot! C'mon, boy!" Josh called from the lawn. When Spot

didn't rouse, Josh called again. "Don't make me come all the way down there. Let's go!"

When the dog still didn't get up, Josh went down to the beach. When he reached down and gave Spot a shake, the dog didn't move.

Chapter Twenty Four

After carrying Spot to the base of the lighthouse and laying him near the shed, Josh went inside to break the devastating news to his wife.

"What took you so long?" she asked.

"Honey, someone shot Spot," he said, his voice shaky. "He's dead."

Madi gasped in horror and Josh wrapped his arms around her. He held her as she sobbed. Words could not express what Spot had meant to their family. If it hadn't been for the loyal dog, they knew what fate Madi would have met at the hands of Thomas Walker Jr. Spot was her shadow, hardly ever leaving her side. He was her office dog, the lighthouse dog, and their son's best friend.

Josh did not let go of Madi. He held his wife, stroking her hair, kissing her forehead, and consoling her as best he could. After a long period of muffled sobs, Madi finally spoke.

"This is no joke, Josh."

Josh nodded, whispering, "I know, Madi—I know."

* * *

Early Wednesday morning, through swollen eyes, the couple selected the location where they would lay Spot to rest. It was at the base of the lighthouse opposite the stairs, overlooking Spot's favorite place to roam the beach. They were exhausted from lack of sleep, both of them on edge all night at the sound of any movement. Josh had a patrol car stationed outside their home, as well as the house where Noah was staying. He had placed a third car at the elementary school that morning.

Josh was awaiting a call from the Maine State Prison. After he'd found Spot, Emily had placed an emergency call to the warden, stating their urgent need for a meeting with Bill Andrews. Josh needed to find out how Andrews had orchestrated this, and put a stop to him before another member of his family got hurt. Andrews had tried to scare Josh and his family before, most recently following a failed parole hearing three years prior. In the past, his intimidation had come in the form of a phone call, in which an unidentified voice would simply say, "When I get out, you'd better watch your back."

Andrews had always denied making the calls to Josh's family, and the blocked number was untraceable. But at trial, the man had blamed Josh for his actions, insisting that he had been coerced into killing his ex-wife's lover, Robert Peterson. If the sheriff hadn't led him to believe that the scumbag had killed Kay, Andrews wouldn't have avenged her death by killing the son of a bitch. His story had not convinced the judge, and Andrews was convicted of second-degree murder.

This was the first time that Andrews had mailed anything to them, or committed such a callous crime against Josh's family.

The ground was cold and more rock than dirt. It took Josh over an hour to dig the grave, and it was an effort even for him. They each said good-bye to Spot, and Madi planted colorful mums atop the grave. As they stood there staring out at the sailboats on Penobscot Bay, they talked about Noah and what they would tell him. They agreed to wait until they could bring him home and share the news together as a family. They had no idea what they would tell him about how Spot had died.

Madi had arranged with Kendyl late the night before for Noah to stay at least another night with them, or until Josh could be sure they would be safe at the light keeper's cottage.

Josh thought this nightmare was over long ago, when he'd put Andrews in prison. There had been no parole hearing the last two years, as he would have been notified of them, so why now? Why was this happening?

* * *

Josh answered the phone to a crazed Emily.

"Those stupid fucking assholes!" she said. "They fucking let Andrews out two months ago and didn't fucking inform us!"

The hair on Josh's neck stood up like a rabid dog. Andrews was out. *That's impossible,* he thought. It had only been eight years. His sentence was ten to fifteen.

"Out on fucking parole," Em continued. "Really? Really?"

Josh couldn't believe what he was hearing. While trying to maintain his own composure, he worked to calm Emily down. Somehow in spite of their emotions, they managed to brainstorm some strategies for pinpointing Andrews's whereabouts, and agreed to meet at the station in fifteen minutes.

He explained the situation to Madi, and then told her he was going to drop her off at Kendyl's before meeting up with Emily. His anger was rising, and Madi could hear it in his voice.

"We're going to find him," Josh said, "and he's going to wish he never met me."

"Josh, calm down," she told her husband as he drove like a maniac toward her friend's house. Josh didn't have a violent bone in his body—that is, until eight years ago. Now if anyone even looked sideways at his wife or son, he would lose his cool.

"I'm not going to calm down until I find that piece of shit and show him who he's dealing with. That bastard shot Spot."

"I know, Josh, but your son doesn't need a father in prison. This guy is not worth going to jail for."

"No one will ever know what I did with him," Josh replied adamantly.

"Joshua Frances Daniels, I know you don't mean that. I am *not* going to be the wife of a convicted felon, or worse, a widow. Please, think of your son," she pleaded, begging him to calm down.

"I'll be fine, Madi, don't worry. I've got it under control," he answered, dropping her off and giving her a quick kiss. "I'll call you later. Stay here, and don't go anywhere tomorrow after Noah gets back from school."

As she watched him drive off, she said a silent prayer for her husband to stay safe and not to do anything crazy.

* * *

His plan was going exactly as scheduled. After he watched them bury their dog from the other side of the lighthouse, he headed back to Mahalas Lane to wait for his next move.

Soon he would have the cottage all to himself. He'd waited a long time for this. He only wished his mother were alive to see it.

* * *

Emily and Josh sat in front of Warden Richardson and listened to her explain that Bill Andrews had been transferred to the Bolduc Correctional Facility in Warren three years ago, following his parole hearing. He had spent five years at the state prison before moving down the road. He was placed in a minimum-custody dorm where he worked in the metal shop, making license plates for the state of Maine. After two years working for the State and participating in the Alcoholics Anonymous Furlough Program, he was sent to the Central Maine Pre-Release Center a little over twelve months ago.

"Six months back, he was enrolled in their work-release program," the warden explained. "Then, seven weeks ago, he was released on probation."

"Why wasn't my department notified of any of this?" Josh asked in disbelief.

"I have no idea, Sheriff Daniels. This was out of my jurisdiction. Once he left Bolduc, he was no longer my inmate."

"We need to know where he is and the name of his probation officer," Emily demanded.

The warden rose and instructed them to remain in her

office while she located the information they needed.

"This is fucking bullshit!" Em spewed at Josh.

"Easy on the F-bombs, Em—the little one can hear you," Josh reprimanded as he pointed to her enlarged midsection.

"I don't give a fu—." She stopped short as the door opened and the warden returned.

"Here is his current address and the department where he reports to his P.O.," she said, handing them a piece of paper, adding, "He reports in every two weeks. I hope this helps."

They shook hands with the warden and thanked her for her time. As they exited her office, she offered one last piece of information.

"Andrews was very disgruntled when he got here. It took about four years before he took advantage of the rehabilitation programs we offer. Before that, he had quite a few problems with his cellmates, and ran his mouth quite a bit. We worked hard to help him see how he could turn his life around. You know, it's never too late."

As soon as they got to the squad car, Emily began her tirade about the warden's "everyone can be rehabilitated" mantra. Em's theory was that if it looks like a duck and quacks like a duck, it's a fucking duck. Some seeds were just bad, and no amount of rehab would ever change that.

They sped down coast to Portland and the Adult Community Corrections Office to see one Louis Eduardo, probation officer.

* * *

Only a couple hours remained until Noah got out of school, and Madi needed to pull herself together. Her head was throbbing, her nose was stuffed up, and the tears wouldn't stop flowing. She loved Spot so much, and now he was gone. She couldn't contain her emotions for more than a few minutes at a time.

When Kendyl returned home from volunteering at the school, she did her best to comfort her distraught friend. After watching Madi move her lunch around the plate for a while, Kendyl took it from the table and made her some hot tea. She insisted Madi take the tea and go lie down for a while, and excused herself to her home office.

Madi knew a nap was not going to happen as she lay on Kendyl's guest-room bed, staring at the ceiling. Instead, she decided to call Kristen. She needed to let Kris know what was going on before she and her family arrived on Friday.

"Do you still think we should come?" Kristen asked.

"I don't know, Kris. I guess we have to wait till Josh gets back from seeing Andrews," Madi answered somberly. "He might say you can't come."

Kristen understood, but knew her old friend needed her.

"You and Noah should come to New York for a while," Kris said. "You can stay with us. Josh won't want you two in any more danger."

"We'll see . . . I can't even think straight. How could Andrews kill our dog when he's in prison?" The tears began again.

"He's crazy, Mad. He wants revenge. I've been telling you that for years. You should have moved out of Maine a long time ago."

This was something Madi had heard frequently from her New York friends and family. Each time, she would explain that Walker was dead and Andrews was behind bars.

"The few threats we've gotten from Andrews have been harmless," Madi said.

"Until now," Kristen replied.

"Yeah, I guess you're right."

"I'm so sorry, Mad. I love you, honey, and I'm here for you. If you want me to come up right now without the family, I will. Just say the word."

"Thanks, Kris. I'll let you know."

They hung up and Madi closed her eyes. Noah would be off the bus soon, and she needed to rest her burning eyes for just a minute.

CHAPTER TWENTY FIVE

When Madi didn't answer her cell phone, Josh tried Kendyl's house. Kendyl explained that the boys had gotten home safely from school, but Madi hadn't stirred for over two hours.

"She cried all night," Josh explained. "Didn't sleep a wink."

"I can imagine," Kendyl replied. "She's heartbroken over that dog."

Josh told Kendyl what they had learned about Andrews's release. He explained that extra patrol cars were all over Owls Head and were watching her house. He wanted Kendyl to ask her husband to come home until Josh could get Madi and Noah relocated. He didn't want to place their family in any danger.

"I don't want any of you in danger either, Josh."

"Thanks, Kendyl. I'm sorry about all this. I'll call you back in a while."

She hung up with Josh and immediately called her husband. At this time of day, it would take him nearly an hour to get home from his office in Camden. She couldn't believe this was happening in her quiet community, and she was scared to death for Madi and Noah. Madi had to be told what was going on.

She double- and triple-checked all the doors and windows while the boys played air hockey in the finished basement. She could hear them laughing. They hadn't a clue what the adults right above them were going through.

While she hated to wake her, Kendyl knew Madi would be furious if she let her sleep while Bill Andrews was out there somewhere. She would want to have her eye on Noah every second.

Once Madi was awake and they had talked, the two friends looked out the huge bay windows in the living room and spotted the officers on either end of the road. Then they went to the basement to keep busy with the boys.

"Who's up for a game of moms versus kids?" Kendyl asked energetically as she and Madi descended the steps armed with huge, fake smiles.

"Me!" they screamed in unison.

"Bring it on," Grayson challenged, and the boys high-fived each other in delight.

* * *

An hour and a half later, the two officers were sitting in the tiny lobby of a plain brick building on Washington Avenue in Portland, waiting to meet with Andrews's parole officer.

"Hello, I'm Officer Eduardo," he introduced himself upon entering, offering Josh his hand, then Emily. "C'mon back."

They followed him to an even smaller room on the other side of the reception wall and sat in metal chairs crammed opposite the desk.

"What can I do for you this afternoon?" he asked.

Josh explained that they were looking for information on Bill Andrews and anything he could tell them about his recent activities. He told him that he'd been the arresting officer, and gave the P.O. a full history of the case. He also told Eduardo about the card they'd received in the mail, and the shooting of their dog the night prior.

Eduardo said he would be surprised if Andrews had had anything to do with the recent events, since he had come in for his scheduled visits, was attending a support group in Portland, and was reporting to work regularly. Andrews did not have his own vehicle, and used the city bus for transportation.

"His boss is supposed to contact me if he doesn't show. We keep a tight eye on everyone in the work-release program."

Andrews was due in the next day, as he was required to physically check in at the office every two weeks. Eduardo had last seen him two Thursdays ago.

"Would you please call his workplace and ask if he's been at work all week?" Emily asked.

The officer assured them that he had, but complied and dialed a number he pulled from his Rolodex. Andrews was working as a welder at a shipyard in Portland, one that employed many of the state's work-release candidates. He spoke with the foreman for a few minutes and then concluded his call.

"I see . . . All right. Thanks, Spencer." He hung up and looked at them both for a moment before speaking.

"It seems as though Mr. Andrews was not feeling well and left early today. They didn't think to call me for an early dismissal. It was one o'clock, and he usually gets out at three.

They do expect him in tomorrow," Eduardo continued, "and he has to meet with me afterwards for his four o'clock appointment. I can arrange for you to go to the yard in the morning to meet with him, or you can come here tomorrow afternoon."

It was apparent the P.O. didn't understand that Josh wanted a faster response time.

"I'm not sure if you are fully aware of the gravity of the situation," Josh said firmly. "Andrews has made threats to my family in the past, and I believe he shot and killed my dog. I have officers guarding my family, and I need your assistance in arranging a meeting with Andrews—*now*."

The P.O. stood up, gave Josh a good long stare, and excused himself to another room. Josh and Em heard a door open and close, and they looked at each other in bewilderment.

"Did he just leave?" Em asked.

"I'm not sure. Let's give it a minute," Josh replied.

Exactly three and a half minutes later—Emily timed it— they heard the back door open and within seconds, the officer reappeared before them.

"I have a squad car on its way to Andrews's place. It's a small studio in South Portland near the shipyard. They will call when they confirm he is home. We can drive together, or you can follow me there," he said as he sat back in his chair.

"Thank you," Josh offered gratefully.

"I apologize for stepping out so abruptly," Eduardo said. "I never like to hear that one of my men might be snowing me."

"Understandable," Josh replied.

As they waited, Eduardo asked some more questions about the past events in Owls Head. When Josh got to the part about the cottage and the Walker case, Eduardo looked at them oddly.

Catching the expression, Josh asked, "Did I say something peculiar?"

The officer replied, "I only have his case file, which says he killed his ex-wife's lover outside a bar in Rockland. I know Andrews has a problem with the sauce, and understood the murder to be a drunken rampage that went south. I didn't know about the other murder case. He's never mentioned the Walker fellow."

Emily asked, "What resonates with the Walker case and Andrews?"

"Well, when you mentioned Owls Head, I just remembered something. Andrews told me during a recent visit that when he finishes his work release next year, he's moving to Owls Head to live in a cottage near his ex-wife's house. Didn't think anything of it at the time."

"Why would he move there?" Emily asked, perplexed.

"He had some money from an inheritance before he went to prison, and had found a partner to invest in some real estate. Said it was a great deal. He said something about it being this guy's family home," Eduardo explained. "I thought maybe—"

"Nah," Josh interrupted. "It can't be the same guy, or the same house. Walker is dead."

"Oh," the officer said. "Are you sure?"

"I put a bullet through his head. I'm sure."

Emily added, "But neither of us wants that asshole living anywhere near Owls Head."

The phone on the desk rang loudly, interrupting their conversation. Eduardo picked it up, listened for a minute, and then instructed his officer to remain outside Andrews's apartment until he arrived. "If Andrews tries to leave, tell him

I'm stopping by for a visit," he added.

Hanging up the phone, Eduardo looked at the two officers and said, "He's there. Let's go."

* * *

From the squad car, Josh called and checked in with Madi. She and Kendyl were doing their best to entertain the boys and at the same time, distract themselves. She was relieved to hear that Andrews was at his apartment in South Portland, and Josh was on his way to see him. Hopefully he would be arrested, and this nightmare would be over so they could all return to the lighthouse.

Josh planned to get Andrews to admit to the dog shooting so that he could be remanded back to Bolduc and kept away from his family. If he couldn't accomplish this, he would return to Andrews's place without the P.O., or Emily, and scare the living bejeezus out of him. One way or another, he would make sure Andrews stayed away from them for good.

Eduardo knocked on the dilapidated door of the run-down apartment near the railroad tracks.

"Bill, it's Officer Eduardo. I need to speak with you," he called through the door.

After a minute, Andrews swung open the door, welcoming his P.O. with a big smile, "Hey, man, what the heck are you doing here?" He stopped short the second he caught a glimpse of Josh. His demeanor changed from relaxed to tense upon seeing his nemesis.

"What the fuck is he doing here?" Andrews asked his probation officer.

Eduardo answered with a firm but gentle response. "Bill,

he's just here to ask you a few questions. Let us in."

Eduardo knew his clients well enough to know that while his job was to make sure they were staying out of trouble, it took a certain level of trust between them to get inside their heads. He always treated his clients with respect, which in turn was usually returned with cooperation.

Andrews looked between Josh, Emily, and his P.O. for a few moments while deciding whether to open the door and allow them in or slam it in their faces. Eduardo had done right by him up until now, helping him get his job and his apartment. But the last time he'd had any dealings with the sheriff of Owls Head, he had been driven to the point of rage and killed a man. He had spent the last eight years regretting that he had ever heard of Sheriff Joshua Daniels.

"Bill, you need to open the door," Eduardo impressed upon his client. "Now."

Andrews reluctantly pulled back the door and stepped back for them to enter, although what he really wanted to do was beat the shit out of Daniels. Make him suffer for all the years he'd spent in prison.

They all stood inside the doorway with the front door still open. Andrews could see there was a Portland police car parked across the street, with two more cops inside.

"What do you want from me?" he asked defensively, wondering what had brought all these uniforms to his shitty little hellhole. He was getting uneasy real fast.

Eduardo asked Andrews if he had any weapons on him, or in the apartment. When he replied that he didn't, the officer asked him to turn around and place his hands on the round table by the tiny kitchen counter so he could check his body for concealed weapons. Andrews grudgingly agreed, knowing full well that denying the P.O. would get him a ride to the nearest station.

Once they got that out of the way, Eduardo had Andrews sit at the table.

Josh spoke next. "I want to know your whereabouts for the last forty-eight hours. Every detail," Josh demanded, still on his feet.

Andrews looked at each of them and said, "Look, I don't know what the fuck you're after, Daniels, but I'm not your guy. I'm clean. I've been working and going to my check-ins like I'm supposed to." Then he looked at Eduardo and asked, "Didn't you tell them?"

Eduardo answered, "I did. But it seems there have been a couple incidents up in Owls Head that concern the sheriff. Why did you leave work early today, and where did you go?"

"I had a migraine. I came straight home to sleep it off. Now you're giving me a bigger headache, so get the fuck out of my house." He directed that last sentence straight at Josh.

Emily spoke this time, slamming her right hand down on the table. She was too hormonal and annoyed to be dealing with this scumbag again. "You'd better start telling the fucking truth, Andrews, or you're going to be very sorry we showed back up in your life. Your dreams of living the high life up in Owls Head are over. You are going back to prison."

Andrews glared at her and raised his voice. "Listen, you little bitch—just because you put me in jail eight years ago doesn't mean you get to come into my house and fuck with me. You ruined my life once, and that's enough. Leave me the fuck alone!"

The probation officer didn't like the direction this was heading in. He was surrounded by three people who had a long and unpleasant history with each other, and he needed to diffuse this situation, pronto.

"All right, everyone, let's take a deep breath," he said, moving around the table toward Andrews. "Bill, why don't you just tell the sheriff where you've been the last few days so they can be on their way back to Owls Head. The sooner you do, the sooner we'll be out of here."

"I haven't been anywhere near fucking Owls Head. I work, go to AA, and come home. Every day. Just me enjoying my little slice of fucking heaven here in South Portland," he said sarcastically.

"Well, then, you won't mind us taking a look around, right, Mr. Clean?" Emily asked.

"Have a big time," Andrews responded, waving his hand around the cramped one-room studio.

While Josh and Emily looked around for signs of a gun or any evidence of Andrews having mailed the card to Noah, Eduardo sat at the table with his client in silence. Andrews just shook his head at his probation officer in disgust.

After finding nothing, Josh came back to the table, bent forward with both hands on the tabletop, and pushed his face within inches of Andrews's.

"I know you're up to your old tricks. You killed my dog and scared my family. I will make sure you never set foot in Owls Head again. You hear me?"

"I don't give a shit about your family or your damn dog. I wouldn't waste my time on you. Now, like I said, leave me alone," Andrews snarled in return.

Eduardo was standing now, too, with one hand on each man's chest. This was as far as this was going for today.

"We're leaving, Bill," said Eduardo. "I expect to see you

tomorrow at four, and don't let me find out you're a no-show at work. That patrol car will remain there until I'm sure you aren't going anywhere but Portland and back. "It's time to go," he stated to Josh and Emily.

On their return drive, Eduardo assured the two officers that he and his department would keep track of Andrews and wouldn't let him out of their sight.

"There is no one else besides Andrews who would know about the note or what was written in it. It wasn't admissible at his trial. Only he, the attorneys, and the judge know the details of the Walker case and how the cases were connected," Josh told the P.O. "I don't believe him for a second, but I'm going to trust you to keep him under wraps for now—until I can find the evidence to put him back up in Warren."

CHAPTER TWENTY SIX

The cottage in Cushing was owned by the Farnsworth Museum and was located near the Olson House, on Davis Cove. An inlet located behind Tenants Harbor and Port Clyde, Davis Cove had just a scattering of homes and was extremely private.

Josh had arranged with his mother to rent the cottage for the upcoming weekend. Since it was a holiday and the Olson House was closed, the cottage would be empty. It was used exclusively to house artists, serious art collectors, and gallery dealers who were in town for special occasions, shows, and events at the museum.

There was no possible way Andrews could know about this place. Josh saw this as an extra precaution over the next few days, while Kristen and her family were visiting.

He didn't tell his mother anything about Andrews, or Spot. He simply told her that he thought it would be fun for the kids to stay there for the weekend, and that the idea had popped into his head at the last minute.

Madi called Kristen on the way back to the lighthouse.

She left Noah at Kendyl's while she went to pack. Noah was still in the dark about the dog, and he didn't yet know they were heading to Cushing. Noah had visited the Olson House on occasion with his grandmother, on museum business, and he would be thrilled to stay there. They would tell Noah that dogs were not permitted, and that Spot was being watched over the weekend by Lynne Hardy's daughter, Taylor.

Taylor was the oldest child of the owners of the general store. Prior to leaving for college, she had been Noah's favorite babysitter. A nursing student at the University of Maine, she would be in town for the long Easter weekend. She was engaged to Michaela's son, Damian, and came home to see him as often as she could.

"Since Josh has Bill Andrews under surveillance, why do we have to stay at some rustic cabin in the woods?" Kristen asked, disappointed at not being near the lighthouse and the attached beach on the bay. She knew Cushing was even more rural than Owls Head, if that was even possible.

Madi laughed. "It's not rustic, Kris, and it's not in the woods. It's right on the cove. It's owned by a world-renowned museum, and it's really nice. They use it to impress art buyers. Trust me. It has four bedrooms and a huge yard that the kids will love. They can fish off the dock. I'll take you on a puffin tour—you'll love it."

"Yay, puffins," her friend replied drily. "The things I do for you, Mad."

"You can help Josh and me come up with a good story to tell Noah about how Spot died. I don't want him to know the dog was shot."

Kristen reluctantly agreed.

"You're the best, Kris," Madi said, and with a brief

good-bye, she hung up with her friend.

While she gathered some clothes for Noah, Madi thought about what Kristen had said in their last conversation. Her friend was right; she *was* always asking Kristen to come to Maine to visit. She hadn't been back to New York in almost three years. Had it really been that long? She promised herself that she'd plan a visit to Kristen in the city before the year was over.

Noah would sleep over at Grayson's that night, and they would leave in the morning for Cushing.

* * *

"What the fuck is going on up there, Fletcher?" Bill barked into the phone the second Glen Fletcher answered.

"Bill! Hey, buddy, not much. What's new with you?" the man responded.

"I'm not playin'. You messin' with the Daniels family again?"

"No, no, not at all. Why, what's the word?" he asked, acting concerned.

"Gee, where do I start? Someone sent their little brat a fuckin' birthday card that said, *It's mine.* Then, umm, let's see . . . someone shot their goddamn dog!" Bill yelled, adding, "I'm not goin' back to prison because you want to play your silly games."

Fletcher tried to calm him down. "Easy does it, Bill. I'm telling you, I haven't been anywhere near the Daniels family. Not since I bought cookie dough from the kid when they came to my door selling it for school. That was months ago. Relax, my friend."

"Look, I'm a year from being free of this shitty-ass job and this crappy apartment. I gave you a lot of money. You better not fuck with me," Bill said.

"We're all good, Bill. I'm lying low till you get here," he said. "But you better figure out who's really messing with them, or you're gonna be screwed."

Bill felt relieved to hear his partner hadn't been involved . . . sort of. Glen was right; he needed to keep his name clean, or he would never get to retire to the cottage. After all he had done to turn his life around, he didn't need to be accused of another crime he hadn't committed, like he had been with Kay's murder. He just wanted to get a small boat and spend his days catching a few lobsters to enjoy on the front patio of the cottage. Was that too much for a run-down old salt to ask for?

* * *

The Olson House guest cottage was amazing, inside and out. It amused Madi that regardless of the size or grandeur of a house in Maine, it was always called a cottage. To her, that meant small, like a studio or one-bedroom apartment. This home, however, was spectacular. There was a small wooded area with shaded picnic tables near the garden, as well as close to the road, making the house invisible to passersby. Of course, the acre-sized garden was professionally maintained and straight off the pages of *Coastal Living*. New spring flowers had just been planted, and with any luck, the snowfall was over for the year. The water frontage was nearly four hundred feet, and there was a private dock and mooring. Granted, it might be a little chilly outside for Kristen's kids, but Noah was a Maine native, like his dad.

From the western-facing decks were panoramic garden and ocean views. Inside, the gigantic family room had an A-framed wall of glass windows from floor to ceiling, boasting the same expansive views. The room was decorated with neutral tones to match the stone and sand of the water's edge. Madi planned to spend much of her weekend on the endless decks and the sprawling beige leather sectional in the family room in front of the fireplace. She imagined the stars and moon could light up this room without a single lamp being on.

Noah was in his glory. Grandma had taken him here once or twice when she'd come by to drop off information for the guests who were staying here, but he'd never gotten beyond the front door before.

As soon as Madi and Josh began unloading the car, Noah was off to the backyard with his fishing pole. Madi knew he would be out there for hours, giving her time to unpack before Kristen arrived the following evening. Josh transferred all the food from the cooler into the kitchen's stainless-steel refrigerator, and marinated steaks for their dinner. He was excited to try out the massive Weber grill on the main deck. Tomorrow, they would have fresh lobster with their guests.

Josh had a few hours of work to get done so that he could take tomorrow and the rest of the weekend off to spend with their company. Once the suitcases and the larger items like the bikes and all the fishing equipment were carried in from the car, Josh kissed Madi and told her to try and enjoy the day with Noah. She was still so emotional about Spot that she was practically walking around in a trance.

"I'll be okay," she told her husband.

"I love you, Mad," he said, staring into her eyes. "More than anything."

"Me, too—more than anything." She gave him a long, hard hug and sent him on his way, adding, "Go say good-bye to Noah on your way out."

* * *

Josh wasn't really going to the office. Emily was off this afternoon, and it was the perfect time to pay Andrews a secret visit. He couldn't get past the note and the dog in the same week, especially so close to Andrews's release. Even if the note had been some sick joke by Andrews, the dog shooting was too much to let go. Spot being shot by some random person in Owls Head was absurd. Combine that with the P.O. mentioning that Andrews owned property in Owls Head, and Josh was certain Andrews was behind these two events.

Andrews is one dumb fool, Josh thought. He just can't put his ego aside and do the rest of his time cleanly. Instead, he's going to let revenge put him in jail for good. Josh would get the truth out of him today, of that much he was certain.

He knew the patrol car wouldn't show up until at least four-thirty, when Andrews returned from seeing Eduardo. So, at three o'clock he parked his car about a mile away and walked to Andrews's apartment. To be sure he wasn't seen, he entered the apartment through a small open window at the rear of the studio. The deserted parking lot was evidence that this complex was primarily working people. He sat at the same round table he had leaned on two days ago and positioned himself against the front wall so that the officers in the vehicle could not see him when Andrews opened the front door. Then, he waited.

* * *

About twenty minutes after Josh left, there was a knock at the front door. Madi looked out the kitchen window and didn't see Noah on the dock. *He must have gone around to the front to come inside,* she thought, knowing that Josh had locked the door behind him when he left.

"I'm coming, sweetie!" she hollered from the kitchen, wiping her wet hands on the towel. She had been making their lunch.

As soon as she'd unlocked the front door, a man in a ski mask shoved it open and grabbed her, instantly twisting her around and covering her mouth. She tried to scream to alert Noah, but couldn't get out more than a muffled gasp. He pushed her against the wall of the family room and handcuffed her hands behind her back with one of his hands. The other elbow was buried into her back, forcing her chest and cheek flush against the wall. He had shoved a rag in her mouth and she couldn't make a sound other than a guttural cry.

How could this be happening again? she thought in terrified disbelief.

He blindfolded her and yanked her away from the wall by pulling upwards on her wrists. She squealed in pain as she complied.

He pushed her forward, out the door, down the front steps, and across the lawn. She stumbled as she searched for footing, and after nearly falling twice more, she found herself in the backseat of a car and heading down the road. She slid herself across the seat to feel if Noah was also in the car, and thankfully, he was not. As tears streamed down her face, she prayed her son was still safe at the cottage, fishing off the back dock.

CHAPTER TWENTY SEVEN

It was nearly five o'clock when the apartment door opened and an exhausted Andrews strolled in. Josh had been waiting for almost two hours.

When Andrews turned to shut the door, he saw the sheriff sitting at the table.

"Just shut the door and don't make a sound," Josh said. Sitting in front of him on the table was his handgun.

Andrews took one look at the weapon and shut the front door.

"Sit down," Josh instructed him, pointing across from the table.

Andrews sat and said nothing.

"Why, Andrews? Why fuck up your life again when you're so close to being done?"

Andrews just stared at him, saying nothing.

Josh went on. "I know you wrote the note, because no one else knows about it but you."

No response.

"And you knew about the dog. You knew he saved my wife's life."

More silence.

"I have proof it was you," Josh said.

After this comment, Andrews began to stir but still said nothing.

"I know you killed the dog, and I know you invested in a house in Owls Head so you could get close enough to me and my family to have your revenge."

Andrews let out a quick laugh.

"But you're too stupid, Andrews. Your brain is fried from all those years on the boat, and in the bottle." Josh pulled out a pen from his pocket with a napkin and waved it in front of Bill.

"See this, Andrews? This is your pen, with your fingerprints. I'm going to place this pen on my property. Then your beautiful life here in the projects will be over."

Andrews stood up from the table slowly, his face red as a beet. Josh placed his hand on the gun. Andrews spit on the table near the gun, and said, "You don't know shit, Daniels. You're the stupid one."

Before Andrews could stop himself from losing his temper, it was too late. *He's getting the best of me again,* Bill thought. *Don't let it happen. Think of your program. Think of your freedom. Maintain control.*

Josh's cell phone rang. It was Madi. He needed to answer it, but didn't want to lose control of this situation.

"Sit down," he commanded Andrews, grasping his gun and then answering his phone. "Madi?"

"Hi, Daddy." It was Noah.

"Well, hey, bud. What's up? Where's Mommy?" Josh asked,

still looking straight at Andrews and holding the pistol firmly in his hand.

"I thought she was with you," he answered. "She's not here."

"What do you mean, buddy? She must be there. She wasn't going anywhere."

Josh was now staring at Andrews with a look that clearly said *What did you do with my wife?*

"No, Dad, I looked everywhere. I came in from fishing and she's not here. Her car is here."

"Then she must be there, Noah. Do me a favor—hang up with me and call the station. It's number two on Mommy's speed dial. Tell them you need Emily to come over right away, and stay on the phone with them till she gets there, okay?"

"No, Daddy, I don't want to hang up. I'm scared. Where's Mommy?" Noah started to cry.

"It's okay, Noah," Josh assured him. "Just lock all the doors, okay? Emily will be there soon. Hold on a second, okay, buddy?" He put the phone on mute, stood up and lifted the gun to Andrews's forehead.

Andrews had no idea what was happening, but he knew the sheriff was on the verge of losing it. He had seen that look in prison many times. A man can only be pushed so far.

"Where. Is. My. Wife." Josh uttered the four words from the bottom of his soul, in a growl so deep he didn't even recognize his own voice.

Andrews knew the sheriff wasn't messing around, and he raised his hands in surrender, "I have no idea, man. I swear. No idea."

"You know who killed my dog. And now they have my wife. You are here, so it has to be someone you hired. Spill it, or I'm going to spill your brains all over this shithole."

"Look, I just wanted a house where I could retire."

"What did you do?"

"I just invested with him," he said. "That's all."

"*Who?*" Josh shouted.

"One of my old cellmates. He wanted to go in on a house in Owls Head. He knew I had an inheritance. He needed my money to get the house," Andrews said. "Don't freakin' shoot me, man."

Josh cocked the hammer.

Andrews panicked. Daniels was going to kill him.

"I didn't know. I didn't know who he was until after he bought the house," he confessed. "He wants to kill your family."

"I will ask you this one more time before I kill you, Andrews. *Who is it?*" Josh asked again.

"Fletcher. Glen Fletcher," Andrews blurted out. "Now put the gun down. I'm begging you!"

Who? Does he mean the retired man who had bought the Walker place after the trial? The local media coverage of the two murders had put a big damper on the rental market for several months, and the owner couldn't carry the mortgage, so she'd short-sold it to an older fellow from Ogunquit.

Why on earth would Glen Fletcher want to hurt my family?

* * *

The man lifted her blindfold after she was tied securely to the chair and looked at her, smiling. Madi couldn't see his face, still covered with a ski mask, but she could see his eyes.

She was struck with shock. Surprise. Terror. Those eyes—

she knew them well. *But how? He was dead.*

Then, the ghost of a man pulled off the mask and said, "Mrs. Daniels, let me introduce myself. I am James McNair, half-brother of Thomas Walker Jr. And this is *my* house."

She looked around and recognized the barn belonging to the Walker cottage on Mahalas Lane, the house she'd rented during her first trip to Owls Head. She saw the dusty front window and the pile of boxes that hadn't been moved in eight years. Then, she stared back at the man who stood in front of her—the man she knew as Glen Fletcher, the friendly retiree who was also the current owner of this cottage. This didn't make sense. Why was he saying his name was James McNair?

Half-brother? This is surely a nightmare, and I need to wake up.

She felt faint and the room was spinning. She wasn't herself. Ever since Spot's death, she'd felt dizzy and faint. She hadn't eaten yet today. In fact, she'd almost had lunch ready when she heard the knock at the front door in Cushing. She couldn't speak. The bandana was now a soggy mass in her mouth. She was hyperventilating and starting to lose consciousness.

He slapped her in the face and commanded, "Oh no, you're not going to pass out on me, Mrs. Daniels. I have quite a fantastic story to tell you."

The last thing she saw was his eerie smile, and those dark, soulless eyes.

CHAPTER TWENTY EIGHT

Emily had just fed her daughter dinner when she got the radio call from Josh that Noah needed her at the cottage in Cushing. She threw on her uniform at lightning speed and blew her family a kiss as she dashed out the door.

"Noah, I'm on my way, honey," she called him as soon as she got in her squad car. "Are you okay?"

"Yes, Aunt Emily. Do you know where Mommy is?" he asked, sounding terrified.

"I think she may have run to the store, sweetie," Emily answered hastily. *The store? He was eight, not five. He knows his mother wouldn't just leave the house without telling him. And her car was still there.*

"Umm, actually, Noah, I'm not sure where she is, but don't worry, your dad will find her. I'll be there as soon as I can. In the meantime, I'm sending another officer over there right away. Stay on the line with me until he arrives."

"Okay," the meek voice replied.

Once Emily knew that the officer had arrived, she called

Josh and told him Noah was safe. He thanked her, and filled her in on what had happened.

Josh had left Andrews sitting at the table, still stunned from nearly being shot point blank. Josh had flown out the front door, run around the back of the building, and sprinted toward his car. He was in the car going about a hundred, on his way to the Walker cottage, when Emily called.

"Emily, Glen Fletcher is Walker's half-brother." He dropped it on her like a bomb. "I'm sure he has Madi. You need to get to the Walker cottage right now!"

"On my way!" She turned the car around and headed back north toward Owls Head. Josh was still about thirty miles away. While they each drove like madmen up the winding, one-lane road, he filled her in on Andrews's shocking story.

Josh told her to wait until he got there to go on the property. They needed to go in together.

"I'm almost there," she said defiantly. "I'm not waiting for you."

"Emily Sherman, this is an order," Josh demanded. "There is no room for error here. If they're there, call for backup!"

*   *   *

Madi could see the setting sun through the dirty barn window. Glen Fletcher—or James McNair, or whoever this man really was—pulled up an old wooden chair and sat in front of her. As dizzy as she was, he wouldn't let her remain unconscious. As soon as her eyes closed, he would slap her awake. It was freezing in the barn. She was shaking with cold, hard fear, the kind of uncontrollable shakes she had experienced when she was under anesthesia for Noah's C-section. She could barely pay attention as he began to recount his story.

"My mother was Margaret Walker," he announced.

All Madi could focus on was his eyes. The dark, brooding eyes she had seen in the window and in the cabin on the island all those years ago. How could she not have recognized them before? She had met Fletcher a dozen times or more at community functions. He looked nothing like Walker other than the eyes. This man was much slighter than Walker, and not as square in his facial features.

As she tried to control the nausea that had started, she heard bits and pieces of his tale. He was clearly enjoying telling it.

"She gave me up for adoption as an infant," McNair said. "I am the middle child, between Sarah and Thomas. Her infidelity would have been too apparent if she'd kept me. The timing didn't align with her husband's trips out to sea, so Thomas Sr. would have known that I wasn't his. She hid her pregnancy from the neighbors by compressing her belly with Ace bandages. My sister Sarah was too young to notice."

Madi couldn't believe her ears. She was so light-headed. Every time she started to lose her balance or shut her eyes, he would smack her on the cheek repeatedly like he was playing a drum.

"Stay with me now, Mrs. Daniels. I haven't even gotten to the good part yet." He grinned with anticipation.

"I grew up with a lovely family in Ogunquit. Those poor people didn't know what to do with me. I caused them a bunch of trouble, until they sent me to a fancy boarding school in Massachusetts when I was sixteen. The Cushing Academy. Ever hear of it?"

Madi nodded and moaned. The gag was hurting her jaw.

"I stole a few things from the headmistress—like her innocence—so they sent me to jail," he said, laughing like it was a hysterical joke.

She stared at him steadily and tried to fight off the dizziness. She was seeing double at this point.

"Where I met . . . guess who?" he asked, waiting for a response.

She shrugged, and began to cry again.

"Don't cry, Mrs. Daniels; it's okay that you don't know. I'll tell you who. I met a friend of yours, Bill Andrews." With that, he clapped his hands with excitement and laughed. "Yes, yes, it's true. Blabbermouth Bill was my cellmate. And he told me all about you and your sheriff husband and this lovely cottage here in Owls Head.

"Have you ever heard of ancestry.com, Mrs. Daniels?" he asked her, teasingly. "Did you know you can find out who your relatives are?"

She nodded.

"All I had to do was ask my parents for my real birth certificate from the adoption agency, and voila! I was able to track down my birth mother," he said with delight. "What a coincidence, don't you think? Turns out my mother was a lovely woman from Owls Head. And it also turns out that she was a promiscuous little thing."

Madi's eyes widened as McNair's tone shifted to one of anger.

He went on. "Poor ol' stupid Bill didn't know a thing about who I really was. That is, not until after he gave me all his money to buy this house. What a lovely coincidence to have met my dear, sweet, stupid cellmate!"

He laughed a long while, then paused, placing a finger on

his chin. Madi was starting to dry-heave.

"You know what, Mrs. Daniels, you're not looking so good." He stood up. "Let me take that gag out for you."

He removed the bandana and Madi gasped for air, coughing a few times.

He sat back down and continued without much concern for her continuous heaving.

"Hold on now—you must hear the ending. This is the best part," he told her. "I know all about my brother, and I know your husband shot him dead. That wasn't nice, Mrs. Daniels. Not nice at all. So, here's the last chapter of the story.

"I sent your son the note, I killed your dog, and now I'm going to kill you, and poor old Bill is going to take the rap for it. I've been waiting for him to get out of jail to pull this off. And then, I will live happily ever after in my birth mother's house, courtesy of dear old Bill Andrews.

"The end!" he announced with a smile and a tilt of his head.

Madi leaned forward and vomited on McNair's shoes before passing out in her chair.

Chapter Twenty Nine

It was nearly dark when Emily arrived on Mahalas Lane. Josh would be another twenty minutes. She parked up the lane out of sight of the cottage and got out of her squad car. She walked along the wooded edge between where she'd parked and the Walker place. When she reached the driveway, she crouched down low and peeked around the bushes to get a look at the cottage.

The lights were on and she could see inside. There was no movement in the kitchen. She remained bent down as low as she could, her pregnancy preventing a complete squat. She slowly crept up the driveway toward the front entrance of the house, her gun drawn in front of her. Backing up against the exterior wall, she held her gun flush against her chest and peeked in through the living room windows. No movement. Ahead of her was the two-story barn and behind her was the road.

She moved around the front of the house and looked in the hanging windows to the kitchen, then all the way around the side and rear of the cottage. She reached the back laundry-room door and found it unlocked, so she cautiously entered and did a room-by-room search of the first floor, then proceeded to the second. The creaky wooden stairs almost gave her away, and she stopped cold. Waiting and listening, she continued on up the stairs and through the bedrooms. The house was clear.

She checked her watch. Josh was about ten minutes out.

Emily exited through the same door she had entered and crept through the wildflowers to the large barn doors. She slid against the side of the barn to the single door that she knew existed at the rear. Entering the barn, she crouched down and waited for her eyes to adjust. With the sun down beneath the second-story windows, it was dark inside. She scanned the open space of the barn floor and then raised her head to the loft. At first all she saw were stacks of boxes, some old furniture, and miscellaneous yard equipment. Then her eyes settled on an old chair in the center of the loft. *Is that a scarecrow?*

She slowly moved toward the front of the barn with her weapon raised. As she came around the front of the slouched shape, she realized it was a person. *Oh my God.* She gasped. *It's Madi.*

She climbed up the wobbly wooden stairs and quickly made her way to Madi, who was completely bent over and not moving.

"Madi, Madi," she whispered, searching for a pulse. She tapped her gently. "Madi, wake up. It's me, Em."

Madi slowly regained consciousness and fluttered her eyes until they opened. There was a pool of vomit on the floor in front of her.

Emily roused her, untied her feet, and helped her down the stairs.

"C'mon, we need to get you out of here before he gets back."

At the base of the stairs, she took off her department-issued jacket and helped Madi into it. Then she placed her arm around Madi's back and guided her out of the barn and around the opposite side of the property. They maneuvered through the woods dividing the property lines, toward her squad car. By the time they reached the car, Madi was gathering her wits. Emily placed her in the driver's seat and used her key to remove the handcuffs that were holding Madi's hands behind her back. She gave her some water to sip and the keys to the car.

"Noah is safe at the cottage in Cushing, with another officer. Josh is on his way here. I need you to stay in the car, okay?"

Madi pulled herself up in the seat and shook off the dizziness. "Okay."

As Emily was shutting the door, Madi stopped her and said, "Wait—do you know who he is, Em?"

Emily nodded, and Madi told her to be careful.

"I will," Em answered.

* * *

Emily walked back to the driveway of the cottage and saw Josh's car. She gave the driveway and front yard a once-over, but didn't see him. She looked at her silenced radio and saw that he had beeped her a few minutes ago. She quickly called for backup and a squad car to retrieve Madi from her vehicle.

The lights were still on inside the house. She did a quick pass around the perimeter and didn't see anyone inside. Had Josh gone to the barn?

She retraced her footsteps from her first search, although this time, it was nearly dark. The moon was lighting up a good portion of the lawn, where there wasn't a cluster of trees. The woods behind the house and barn were speckled with moonlight between the massive firs.

She stepped inside the barn and whispered for Josh. There was no sign of him. She exited the barn and walked across the back lawn to the beginning of the wooded parcel at the rear of the house. The moonlight was streaming through the trees, enough for her to see about ten feet in front of her. She examined the woods as she walked farther back on the property.

Suddenly she heard a noise to her right and shifted direction. Where there was a gap in the trees, she made out a male figure bent toward the ground. As she watched, he stood up, and she could see it was McNair, holding a shovel. He was digging.

She stepped closer, staying hidden among the trees, and moved close enough to see Josh lying motionless on the ground beside the man. She moved within fifteen feet of him and positioned herself with an unobstructed line of fire.

"Hold it right there, McNair," Emily called out. "Put the shovel down and let me see your hands."

He dropped the shovel to the ground and put his hands down by his sides, replying, "Well, well, well . . . if it isn't the sheriff's trusty sidekick."

"Let me see your hands," she commanded again.

"You're just in time to join the party," he said, chuckling.

"I guess I'm going to have to dig a bigger grave."

She stepped forward and cocked her weapon, announcing, "Last chance—let me see your hands."

McNair lifted his hands, but in the dim light Emily wasn't able to see that he had a gun in his right hand. He clasped his hands together and cocked his weapon directly at her.

"Drop it, McNair!"

He lowered the gun gently, and Emily thought he was going to drop it to the ground. Instead, he aimed it straight for her bulging belly and she heard the shot ring out.

She gasped as she instinctively reached down for her belly, trying to protect her unborn baby. Almost simultaneously, she saw McNair's head jerk sideways as he crumpled to the ground. It took her a second to realize she wasn't the one who had been shot. She twisted immediately to her right and lifted her weapon toward the direction of the gunfire.

"Drop the gun!" she called out to the darkened figure standing twenty feet to her right.

She walked toward the shooter, who had dropped the weapon and stood motionless. Within ten feet she could see who it was.

"Madi?"

Madi started to sob but didn't move an inch. She just stared at the two men lying on the ground. "Is it . . . ?" she asked, breathless.

She and Emily ran to Josh.

"Josh!" Madi cried out as she reached his fallen figure and fell to her knees. "No! Please no!" she shook him as Emily checked for a pulse. Madi's whole life flashed in front of her. This man, the man she loved, the man she had made the most amazing life with, could not be gone.

CHAPTER THIRTY

The CT scan hadn't detected any brain lesions, and Josh was diagnosed with only a grade-three concussion. Miraculously, there were no hematomas. Bed rest and some follow-up tests were all he needed.

Kristen and her family had arrived Friday night as scheduled, and Josh was conscious by the time they made it to the hospital to see him. He had only remained unconscious for a few hours, which the doctor said was a good sign. He didn't remember being struck by McNair's shovel or being dragged into the woods. He also had no recollection of his wife gunning down the man who had tried to kill them.

Not long after they were married, Josh had taken a resistant Madi to the shooting range, insisting she learn how to shoot. Prior to that, she'd been deathly afraid of guns, and wouldn't even allow Josh to bring his into the house.

The training had paid off. Madi had found Emily's spare weapon in her glove box and used it to save Josh's life.

At the hospital, Madi was thoroughly examined, and the

doctor shared the news with them once Josh was awake. The dizziness and nausea weren't due to stress or overwork. She was pregnant! They were surprised and delighted. Noah was also fine, and thrilled to learn he was going to be a big brother.

Josh convinced the doctor to release him on Sunday morning so he could spend the holiday with his family. They decided to go ahead and stay at the rented house in Cushing to enjoy the spectacular setting for their Easter dinner. Madi picked up Josh from the hospital around noon, and when they arrived at the sprawling cottage, they were greeted by all of their closest friends and family. Madi had arranged the gathering to celebrate Josh's recovery and to share their big news.

With every opportunity their friends had out of earshot of the children, Madi and Josh answered in detail the onslaught of questions surrounding the events that had taken place at the Walker cottage. The couple decided to wait until the inquisition had died down before making their announcement.

Seating himself at the head of the table, with Madi on his left and Noah on his right, Josh called for everyone's attention. "Before we eat, I'd like to make a toast." Glasses were raised, and Josh began once the group fell silent.

"Many of you knew me before I met Madi," he said. "You also know what a difference she's made in my life." He smiled at her sweetly and continued. "Without her, my life would be so boring. It's true—if it weren't for Madi, I would spend my weekends, you know, watching TV, fishing, working around the house . . ."

Where was this going? Madi thought, tilting her head at her husband.

"But instead, I chase murderers up and down the coast. So thank you, Madi," he teased, "for giving my life meaning." He bent over and kissed his wife, and she jokingly gave him a little smack across the cheek. Their friends began to laugh along with Josh.

"Very funny, honey," Madi scolded Josh. "Now do the real toast, please."

"Oh, the real toast? That's right," Josh said. "I almost forgot . . . We're pregnant!"

The group erupted in hoots and hollers, each getting up to offer their congratulations. When they were all back in their seats, the conversation kept its lightheartedness. Everyone had something to say about Madi's heroism, and a few had some teasing of their own to do.

"Maybe we should make Madi the sheriff, Sheriff," Emily taunted. "She's got a bigger set of cojones than both of us put together. And you know I've got a giant set."

As was customary after dinner was eaten, the kids had grown tired of adult conversation and found their own entertainment elsewhere in the house. As the friends compared the case from eight years ago to this one, they noted the irony in the outcomes.

Rick, Michaela's husband, pointed out the strange similarities. "Now that I think about it, Josh and Madi both took a blow to the head at the hands of a crazy man, and they each shot a man to save the life of each other's best friend. If that isn't kismet, I don't know what is."

"You two are like the dynamic duo," Kristen joked. "Like the old show, *Hart to Hart.*"

"More like Cagney and Lacey," Valerie's husband, Joel, chimed in.

"Starsky and Hutch!" Kendyl yelled.

Her husband Stephen added, "I was thinking Crockett and Tubbs from *Miami Vice.*"

And the joking went on. Josh and Madi took it all in stride. They were simply grateful that the nightmare was over, and that they were sitting there among their dearest friends.

As it turned out, Bill Andrews had kept his nose clean after all, other than having the bad luck of befriending a man who took all his money and tried to set him up for murder. Josh had already spoken with Officer Eduardo, and Andrews would be forbidden to step foot in Knox County ever again. Andrews had no problem with that at all, never wanting to see the sheriff of Owls Head again for as long as he lived. The Walker cottage would be sold, and Andrews would retire somewhere far from the coast of Maine.

As the evening went on, Madi looked around the table, tired, but so thankful to have these wonderful people in her life. However, she couldn't help wondering if it was time for them to think about leaving Maine. While they had so many incredible memories here, there were also some that took the charm right out of Owls Head.

Over dessert, the group toasted Josh, Madi, and Noah's safety, and the future arrival of the next Daniels baby.

Madi leaned over to kiss her husband, and asked him loudly enough for all to hear, "Honey, can we move to New York City now? I think it might be safer there."

Which sent the table roaring with laughter once again.